HER DIRTY DETECTIVES

MIKA LANE

HEADLANDS PUBLISHING

ORLA FELLOWES

"Hey. Excuse me. You need to leave now."

He stirred, made a little snore, and turned over.

In my bed. Which he needed to get out of. Immediately.

So, I poked him. Not as hard as I wanted to, but it worked. He grunted and opened an eye, slowly pushing himself up on one elbow and looking around the room—my room—like he wasn't sure where he was.

My hook-up from the night before peered at me, where I stood hovering in my bathrobe, like he expected me to hand him a cup of coffee.

Don't think so.

"Hey," I tried again, "I'm getting in the shower. Please be out of here before I am done. I have a busy day ahead."

His sandy blond hair stuck up in every direction. What was it about guys and bedhead? For a moment I wished I had more time… but I didn't.

Bewilderment washed over his handsome face. "B… but didn't you… I mean, didn't we… you know, have fun?"

Ugh. Just like a guy. Always fishing for compliments when it came to their sexual prowess. And now I had to either soothe him or be a huge bitch and tell him he needed some practice.

Which would be just plain mean, especially since he actually had been pretty good in the sack—actually, *very* good in the sack—but you didn't see me asking for reassurance that my cock-sucking skills were up to par.

"T… Tony, it was a lot of fun. Now, I'm running into the shower. You have a good day. Oh, please don't wake up my stepsister on the way out and feel free to grab a bagel. I think they're on the counter."

I also thought they were stale, but it was the thought that counts.

I patted him on the arm and left, fairly confident

he'd get his ass out of my bed pretty damn fast if he had any pride at all.

Which I was pretty sure he did.

A guy as good looking as Tony—or whatever his name was—usually had plenty of pride. In fact, too much. I knew the type. They walked around, blessed by the universe with their good looks and charm, expecting crowds to part every time they walked into a room.

Not so fast. Personally, I didn't fall for that shit.

I'd only fucked Tony-or-whatever-his-name-was because I was on the rebound. And I think I'd gotten it out of my system. At least I hoped so. One-nighters were kind of stressful.

First, there was the anxiety of bringing a stranger home. I'd taken a photo of T—I'd just call him that—and sent it to my BFF Jenni so that if, god forbid, I ended up missing, she'd have something to take to the police. Then, there was the issue of condoms. What if the guy wanted to be a dick about wearing one?

And last, what if he didn't eat pussy? That would be a total non-starter for me. A dude pulls that with me, and he gets kicked out so damn fast he won't know what hit him.

But there were no such problems with this guy.

At least there wouldn't be if he hit the road like I asked him to before I finished my shower.

Jenni was going to be so proud. Ever since I'd dumped Joey, the last creep I'd dated, she'd been bugging me to 'ho out' as she called it. 'Sow my wild oats,' she also liked to say, by embarking on a hot but meaningless booty binge to remind myself that there were other dudes out there who would find me attractive and who were ten times better than the loser ex.

The loser ex, who was always on to 'the next big thing,' as he put it, sure to bring him riches beyond anyone's wildest imagination. He'd almost gotten my dad to invest in one of his schemes, convincing him that the world needed a better metal detector. He came up with a way to install them in a pair of flip flops so that if you walked on the beach and they started screeching, you could drop to your knees and start digging for your buried treasure right then and there.

The project never got off the ground, and fortunately, my father was saved a lot of money. When my ex had gone for a patent, it turned out someone had beaten him to the idea.

That was a sad day for Joey because he had no backup plan.

But I did. And that was to tell him it was over.

Actually, it had been over for a while. In addition to being a crummy inventor, he was also a crummy human being.

My shower finished, I peeked out of the bathroom to make sure T was gone. My room was empty, thank god, so I slipped down to the front door just to make sure his car was gone, too.

The coast was clear.

I bounded back up the stairs, in a hurry to get to work. My stepsister was probably already there, ready to bitch me out for being late.

Again.

As I hustled to leave eight minutes later, I saw in a pile of mail next to the front door a postcard from my dad and stepmom, on safari in Africa.

I tucked it in my purse to read later.

ORLA FELLOWES

"Hey, Tawny," I said, exploding into the art gallery where she'd given me a job. "I picked up your favorite coffee drink."

I plopped an upside-down caramel macchiato on her desk from the fancy corner coffee shop, expecting a thank you and maybe even a sliver of a smile. I was not above sucking up when I had to.

It was no secret Tawny would rather not have her younger stepsister working alongside her in the town's most successful art gallery. She wanted that baby all to herself. But she didn't have much choice.

My father had backed the venture, and she wasn't about to screw up that sweet ride.

I had to hand it to her. People who benefit from familial *largesse* seldom appreciate it. But, in spite of the fact that she'd been given a massive leg up thanks to Dad, she was really making a go of it. In the short time she'd had the gallery, she'd managed to attract some of the most prestigious and expensive fine art on the market.

And the clients who could afford it.

Amazingly, she'd done it all on her own. Well, and with the help of our parents' connections. Regardless, I had some respect for the woman, even though she couldn't stand my ass.

I didn't care, though. Dad had been through so many wives—which meant I'd been through so many stepsiblings—since my mom had passed that give or take another who loved or hated me didn't mean a goddamn thing. I knew Tawny's mother wasn't going to be in the picture forever. None of them ever were.

But I kept that to myself. If people couldn't see writing on the wall, who was I to point it out?

I waited for Tawny to take a sip of her weird coffee drink. Instead, she looked up at me like she was possessed. And I was to be her next meal.

"What did you do?" she growled, one tiny wisp of hair having escaped from the tight bun she wore every day.

Crap. She knew about the booty call.

I sighed. "You know, Tawny, I'm on the rebound from Joey—"

She narrowed her perfectly lined eyes. Jesus, she was worked up. "Just confess, Orla. And tell the truth."

I glanced at my watch. I didn't really have time to deal with whatever bug was up her ass. I was fifteen minutes away from a client meeting. "Okay. Okay. I had a guy over. It was a good time. He had a pretty big dick and—"

She jumped to her feet and leaned toward me.

I took a quick step back. "Damn, Tawny. Calm down a sec. I'm sorry if you heard us. I really did try to keep the noise down but you know, he just kept—"

"I'm not talking about... that," she said with disgust. "I'm talking about *work*. What did you do here at work?" she snapped.

Work? "I... I haven't fucked anyone here at work."

Her face grew redder, and she slowly shook her head. "I. Don't. Mean. That."

I shrugged. "All right. I drank all the sodas in the fridge. I'll get more at lunch time."

Silly thing to get upset about, but whatevs.

Only she continued shaking her head. "No, not that."

I racked my brains for any other sort of infraction. "I used the copy machine for something personal," I confessed, saying it more like a question than a statement. At this point I was just guessing as to what I'd done that was so bad.

Slam!

Her hand smashed the desk. "Why can't you just be honest? My mother always said you were sneaky."

Well, damn. Two could play that game.

Time for the big guns. "Well, your mother's a witch, and I'm sure my dad will realize that someday."

I'd really poked the bear now. Her nostrils flared.

Actually flared.

And just before I was thinking she might reach out and wrap her hands around my throat, the gallery doorbell rang. Thank god.

I ran to let my client in. My pissed-off stepsister could stew in whatever her problem was. I wanted to make some money off my very first client.

When I'd come to town a couple months earlier, fleeing the wanna-be-inventor boyfriend, Dad had suggested at dinner one night that Tawny take me on as a gallery assistant.

That would be the gallery *Dad* had helped her open.

There was no saying no.

Although the expression on her face indicated that was exactly what she would have liked to have said.

She'd paused her fork, mid-way to her mouth, holding a nice little piece of filet mignon, and side-eyed my father, then looked at her mother, who nodded blankly.

Stepmom didn't give a shit what went on in the household as long as Dad didn't cut off her credit cards.

But Tawny did. "Great idea, but I really don't need any help at the gallery. I'm sure Orla can find something else to do here in town." She turned to me. "Don't you want to go back to teaching kinder-garten?" she asked.

I nodded. "Yeah. Eventually. But I have to apply to the school district and wait until the start of a semester, provided I've been hired. If they don't have an opening in kindergarten, I could consider elementary school, although that would take some preparation—"

"It's settled," Dad exclaimed. "Tawny, you are

working day and night at that place. Don't be too proud to admit you need help."

He reached to pat her head, and I reflexively checked all the knives within her reach.

My stepsister wasn't the 'head patting' type.

But that didn't stop Dad. He was beaming. "I love it. Both our girls working together on a successful venture. That's just what a father loves to see."

"*Step*father," Tawny mumbled, under the scowling eye of her mother.

So here we were, not two months later, and I finally had a client of my own, a dapper older gentleman I'd met at the local garden show. When I'd introduced myself and mentioned the gallery, he said he was in the market for some new pieces for his home and wanted to come by and see the artists we were representing.

"Mr. Dalt, good to see you again."

He took a slight bow. "Miss Fellowes. Lovely to see you. And this is your sister, I presume," he said, turning to Tawny and extending his hand.

Tawny's scowl morphed into a tolerable smile, the kind you gave someone when you had to be nice but really didn't want to.

Cripes, was she an idiot? Couldn't she do better than looking like she'd just sucked a lemon? This man was here to potentially spend money and she was still in a pissy mood.

That was just crazy.

No matter. I handed my client a Perrier, and led him to the first room in the gallery, mostly to escape Tawny's shitty energy.

"Now, Mr. Dalt, we have several abstract-expressionist pieces here, and the next room houses our neo-expressionist works."

Just then, there was a ruckus from the front of the gallery.

"Where is she?" a deep voice demanded.

Mr. Dalt and I looked at each other as two police officers rounded the corner and headed straight for us.

Holy shit. Was Mr. Dalt some sort of criminal? He seemed like such a nice man.

But they weren't there for him.

One of the officers pulled my hands behind my back and the other read me my rights. Mr. Dalt's eyes widened and his bottle of Perrier slipped out of his hand, crashing on our expensive wooden floor.

"Wh… what's going on?" I stammered. "Is this a joke?"

"No ma'am. You're under arrest for art forgery," one of the cops said.

Wait. *What?*

"Art forgery? Me? I don't even know what art forgery is," I cried.

But they led me toward the door in handcuffs, where I could see a patrol car with flashing lights waiting.

The last thing I saw before leaving the gallery was Tawny's face, about as smug as it had ever been.

And that was saying something.

3

TIGE ST. JAMES

"Goddamn, I hate Mondays."

My head was pounding and I hadn't slept worth a shit the night before. It was going to be a long fucking week.

"Hey, loser," Apollo said. "It's not Monday."

I glanced my buddy since childhood, who was pretty much the only person in the world who could call me a loser and not get leveled for it.

He was wearing his usual smirk. For a sensitive guy—self-proclaimed, of course—he sure could be a wise guy.

"What do you mean?" I asked.

"Dude, it's Tuesday."

Well, shit. I dropped my head into my hands in agony. The good news was there were only four days until the weekend instead of the miserable five.

Speaking of miserable, I needed a break. Badly. I'd been working twelve-hour days since I'd taken over my dad's private security firm two years ago. He'd happily retired to Florida with my mother, passing his successful agency on to me. I'd accepted his generous offer with little concept of what it took to run the place, and what it was like to do detective work as a full-time career.

Dad had loved every bit of the work. He really had it in his DNA. I'd thought I did too, having worked off and on for him over the years. I'd just naively never realized that investigating the occasional cheating spouse or providing security for a large event was not the same as being in charge and doing the work day after day.

It wasn't that I didn't like it. No, I relished what the firm's offerings could bring to people's lives. I just needed a break.

And the good news was that my break, my long-planned break, was just around the corner.

"Jesus, you look like shit," Wes said, grabbing coffee from the shitty stuff we kept in the office kitchen.

Great. Another one busting my balls.

"Somebody have a late night?" he taunted.

I caught him and Apollo exchanging a glance. That meant they were about to really lay it on. Which was fine. I could take it. Most days, anyway.

We three had worked together since I'd taken over. I didn't think I could have had a better team of colleagues—and friends.

The downside of that was that they knew my buttons, and just when to push them. Of course, because I knew them so well, it wasn't hard to anticipate when a load of their shit was about to be slung my way.

"Hey, Apollo," Wes said. "I think Tige here got laid last night. Doesn't he have that look about him?"

I braced myself.

Opening my phone's calendar, I checked to see what was on the day's docket. If I ignored the guys, maybe they'd get off my back.

No such luck.

"I think you might be right, Wes," Apollo said. "I think our boy here got lucky. 'Course, he doesn't look too happy about it right now, does he?"

Wes slapped me on the back, and my phone skittered across the table where we were sitting. He and Apollo snickered.

"Apollo, you need to back off, my friend. Doesn't look like Tige is in the mood for our ribbing."

I leaned back in my chair, not willing to let on how much they were irritating me. "It's all good, guys. I'm just gonna grab some of that extra-strength aspirin and wash it down with our delicious coffee."

But Wes stopped me. "Dude. Before you walk away. Got something to share." His face had turned from mocking to serious. Guess it was time to get to work.

I sank back into my seat. "What's up?"

"We got a call from that lawyer friend of yours, Bennie. Turns out a local woman has run into some trouble. He wants you to take the lead on things."

No. Fucking. Way.

Time to lay it out. "Wes, both you guys know I am out of here Friday evening. I've been planning this kayaking trip for weeks, and a meeting with the Dalai Lama couldn't keep me from going. So, you'll have to take the case."

Wes grimaced. "I know, Tige. I know you've been looking forward to this trip. You need a break. Apollo and I both know this—"

"Good," I said. "Then you can get started right away. This week is all about me closing out whatever I have in the works so I can go away and not think for one second about the agency."

Seriously. To say I was longing for the peace and quiet of kayaking in the sunny blue water of the Sea of Cortez was an understatement. I was so out the door, my shit had been packed for days.

I was going to be on that plane, no matter what.

But Wes leaned on the table, wearing what I called his *reasoning* face. I'd seen him use it before. His was a rare skill and it served him well. It served the firm well, too.

Although I was not in the mood for it.

"I don't think we can pass up this job, Tige. It looks like it could get pretty high-profile."

I threw my hands up in the air and returned to getting my coffee. This goddamn headache wasn't going to go away on its own.

"I'm sure you'll handle the case just fine without me. I don't care how much money the woman has. Or how good-looking she is," I said, ending the conversation.

Not so fast.

The guys looked at each other.

"It's not that, Tige. First, Wes and I are booked with that cheating spouse case. All the surveillance is set up. Sure, we could change things, but I wouldn't advise it. Not this time."

"Why the hell not?" I snapped, counting the seconds until the coffee and aspirin kicked in.

"Because this woman is from the Fellowes family."

"What. What?"

Why didn't these assholes start with this bit of important information? The Fellowes were an important local family. My dad was a huge fan.

Before they could answer, I continued. "Why does she need us? What the hell did she do?"

Wes sighed. "That's part of the problem. We don't know much yet. But Bennie called and said he'd helped bail her out, and that if we didn't take the case, we'd be crazy."

"She's already been *arrested*?" I asked.

He and Apollo nodded. "Apparently so. She called Bennie for help. Looks like they're friends from school or something."

I looked out the window to the parking lot where my dad's late-model, diesel Mercedes sat. He'd insisted I take that along with the business. I would have preferred something newer and more reliable. And less noticeable.

I sighed.

And called the travel agency to change my trip.

4

TIGE ST. JAMES

I TURNED FROM MY DESK IN THE BIG OFFICE WE ALL shared. "There. It's done. I hope you're happy now."

Visions of clear blue water, sunny skies, and fish tacos faded into the gray day we were having, the perfect complement to my already-shitty mood.

Apollo rolled his eyes and looked at Wes. "How long do you think he's gonna bitch about this?"

"Dunno, man. But he's really working it. Someone needs to pull up her big girl panties."

Oh, for Christ's sake. "Look. I'll get over it. Let her know she can come over tomorrow. We have a massively busy day ahead of us."

"Um, Tige. That's… not gonna work," Wes said. "Bennie said she is totally fucking freaking out and it needs to be today. But look. I got some more info. It has something to do with… I don't know… art forgery? I mean, I don't know jack shit about that—"

None of us did. All the more reason not to take the case. But it was too late for that.

"Look, guys," Apollo said, "we might not know much about the art world, but this could be a great opportunity to expand what we do. Who knows, could even turn it into some sort of international work at some point. If we did a good job."

Of course we'd do a good job. We never did anything else.

But it was true, we didn't know much about art. Actually we knew nothing about art.

"Got any other info?" I asked.

"The case seems to be focused around that fancy gallery downtown. It's owned by Dominic Fellowes, the woman's father."

I knew the name. Very well.

"So it's his *daughter* who's in trouble?" I asked.

Wes nodded. "It seems so. You know how wealthy people are. Can't seem to play by the rules. I'll bet she's guilty."

Typical Wes. Always expecting the worst. But if I

came from where he did, I'd probably view the world the same way.

"Hey now. I don't think jumping to conclusions will do us any good."

Apollo. The rational peace-keeper. There was a reason why we all worked together so well. I might be in charge, but the firm would be nothing without the perspectives these guys brought to the table.

The office doorbell rang, and Wes jumped up. "Looks like they're here."

They didn't waste any time.

"Hey, bring them into the conference room, will you?" I called after him, deleting my Sea of Cortez screensaver.

No reason to torture myself.

A minute later, Wes let us know our new client—or potential new client—was settled in. I dragged myself out of my chair and tried to shake off my shit mood.

It didn't work.

As with all our meetings, before we started, the three of us took a look through the conference room window, which was mirrored on the other side.

It was something my dad had installed years ago to check out clients before he started a meeting. Sometimes it came in handy.

On that day, I wasn't sure it did. The moment I

looked through the window, it was like someone punched me in the gut.

Twice.

"Holy fucking shit," I mumbled

Wes slapped my back. "Dude. I've never seen you react so strongly to a pretty woman. Are you sure you got laid last night?"

He and Apollo were quite pleased with their teasing.

I put my hands up. "Guys, we cannot take this case. Absolutely not." I started to walk back to my desk.

But Apollo caught up and stepped in my path. "Cripes, Tige, you look like you saw a ghost. What's going on?"

Like I would give them something I'd *really* never hear the end of.

But Wes was smart. *Too* smart. "I know what's going on."

We turned to look at him.

"You know her, don't you?"

God, he could be an irritating fuck.

I glared at him. "Get rid of her. And Bennie, too. This is not going to work. We can't take this client."

Wes got closer, not willing to give up. "Holy shit. This is the girl you slept with last night. Isn't it?"

Apollo stifled a laugh. "No way. This is classic.

Did you know you fucked a girl from the Fellowes family?"

As a matter of fact, I didn't.

Although she did live in a huge freaking mansion on the wealthy side of town. But I'd been thinking with my little head, and had no interest in my surroundings.

"Guys, we gotta ditch this case," I insisted.

But Wes shook his head slowly. "Oh no. Not only are we not gonna ditch this case, but you need to get your ass in there like you said you would and face your… *bootay call.*"

"Yeah, Tige," Apollo chided, "maybe this time you can learn her name."

Both the assholes doubled over with laughter.

But it was all good. If the shoe were on the other foot, I'd be busting both their chops, too.

So not only was my one-nighter sitting right here in my office, she also seemed to have some sort of problem with the law.

"You really know how to pick them, dude," Wes said, opening the conference room door so I had no choice but to enter.

And when I did, let's just say I didn't see happiness in my new client's eyes.

She looked between Bennie and me. "Is… is this a joke or something?"

Exactly what I was thinking.

5

ORLA FELLOWES

"Bennie, I thought you were my friend."

I ignored the detective who'd just joined us, whom my lawyer Bennie had insisted could help me with my little legal... *problem*. I gave him my world-class *I'm gonna kill you* stare.

"Of course I'm your friend, Orla," he said, confused. "What kind of statement is that?"

I looked in the direction of my new 'detective,' who was doing all he could to avoid my gaze, and looked back at Bennie.

"*What?*" he insisted.

I lolled my head back to stare at the ceiling and

clicked my tongue. If that didn't get my message across, nothing would. "You guys are trying to be funny, right? Like funny *ha-ha*?"

He just looked at me.

I thought attorneys were smart. "Bennie, you are my lawyer—"

"Technically I'm not Orla. I helped you get out of jail but we have no formal working agreement—"

"OKAY. Technicalities," I said, waving my hand. "But say if you *were* my attorney, wouldn't it be your job to *be on my side?*"

He frowned, still clueless. "I am on your side, Orla. And I want you to meet Tige St. James."

Ty? What kind of name was *Ty?*

And wasn't his name Tony, anyway?

Still avoiding my gaze, *Ty* passed me a business card. The one he hadn't given me the night before, when we'd spent the night together. That's when I learned *Tige* was pronounced *Ty.*

And people said I had a strange name.

Bennie continued trying to smooth my feathers. "He's the best in town, Orla. Actually, the best in the state. This firm was founded by his father many years ago—"

"That doesn't exactly help me with my current problem, now does it?" I snapped.

He looked between Tige and me and frowned. "Huh?"

"Oh, like you didn't know," I said, crossing my arms.

He looked at the door. Yeah, I bet he was dying to get out of there.

So I continued. "This is no coincidence. I know you guys planned this to set me up. Bennie, who told you I slept with him last night?" I gestured at Tige. "Huh? Tell me."

Tige finally looked my way, horror crossing his face. Bennie wasn't far behind.

I wasn't giving up. "You guys. Pretending to be *so* innocent. Well, I've got your number. And you're full of shit if you think you can throw me off. Bennie, you know full well what I'm talking about, that I fucked that guy sitting right across from us last night."

Bennie's eyes widened. "I… uh… I…"

He apparently hadn't expected me to call him out.

"And you," I said, looking directly at Tige, "are pissed I asked you to leave this morning. Look, buddy, no one wants to do the walk of shame, but it's part of being an adult. And you just had to get back at me. I mean, I had fun, sure. The sex wasn't bad. You know, nothing special—"

At this, both their eyes widened in horror.

Had I gone too far?

I didn't care. "You were pissed I kicked you out, and this is you getting back at me. Brilliant. Clever. Really. Not sure how you pulled it off, but it's not funny. We're talking about my life here."

Bennie's gaze whipped toward Tige's direction. "I thought you had a girlfriend, man."

Tige shook his head. "No, that ended a long time ago."

Okay. So not the point.

Bennie folded his hands on the conference room table and gave me his best trying-to-be-patient look.

"Orla, I brought you here to help you. I know nothing about what you may... have done, or not... done with Tige here, but I left a meeting for you, raced down to the police station, and promised to get the ball rolling on your case since your dad's out of the country."

All that was true.

"So you didn't know..." I gestured between Tige and myself.

"No. And even if I did know, I don't care. That's not why I'm here. That's not why Tige is here, nor is it why you are here. If you don't want my help—or Tige's help—say the word. I know I'm a busy man and I suspect Tige is, too."

He stood to go.

All right. Bluff had been called.

Bennie was the winner.

And I felt like eating a bag of dicks.

"Look, I have a world of shit on my shoulders right now and I was just feeling... defensive, thinking you guys were trying to get one over on me. So fine. Thank you. Thank you, Bennie, for coming to get me this morning, and thank you, Tige —not for last night but for, you know, listening to my... situation."

And for the first time since my life had taken a turn from the lovely new existence I'd created, my eyes filled with stinging tears, tears that had me wondering if leaving the douchebag boyfriend had really been the best idea, wondering if coming back to my old town was smart, and definitely doubting that going to work with my evil stepsister was something I ever should have assumed would work out well.

I should have stuck with kindergartners. They were so much more manageable than grown-ups.

Yeah, I'd been encouraged by Dad to work with Tawny, but I'd always suspected she was trouble. Why I thought things would be any different working together was just a naïve, dumbass move on my part. At least I'd known what I was dealing with in my old life. The boyfriend was a douche, but he was *my* douche, and he was a predictable douche at that.

I'd thought I was so smart to hightail it out of town, like I deserved a better life than an underpaid, underappreciated kindergarten teacher with a drag for a boyfriend.

I should have just stayed in the shit situation I was in. At least that shit was predictable, unlike the shit I was in right now.

6

ORLA FELLOWES

After making a colossal ass of myself in front of my old friend Bennie and new—ah-hem—friend Tige, the long-ass day was coming to an end. Without thinking, I turned my car in the direction of home before I remembered that Tawny lived there too. And I would have to contend with her.

And contend with her, I would. She was a complete and total shit for accusing me of messing with her business, something I barely knew enough about to discuss the difference between neo- and abstract-impressionism, never mind know enough to commit any related crimes.

Art forgery. What the hell was that, anyway?

I made a mental note to Google it as soon as I was home and soaking in my warm, bubbly bathtub.

As I got closer to the house, I took deep breaths. It wasn't going to be easy to see her.

In fact, it wasn't going to be easy to keep myself from strangling her.

Maybe I could avoid her. Dad's house was, after all, pretty huge.

But on the other hand, why should I have to hide out in my own father's house? I'd done nothing wrong. And Tawny was about to find that out.

But when my key wouldn't turn in the front door lock, I started to get worried. I walked around to the garage, where the keypad code didn't work, and then around to the kitchen to see if any of the house-keepers were still there.

I was, for some strange reason, locked out.

But Tawny's car was out front, so I pressed the front doorbell.

"Hello," she sang over the intercom.

Like she didn't know it was me. I looked right up at the security camera and waved.

"Hey, Tawn. I'm locked out. Can you buzz me in?"

I put my hand on the doorknob, waiting for the sound that let me know the door had unlocked.

When it didn't come, I twisted the knob, thinking maybe I'd missed it.

It was locked. Hard and fast.

"Tawny, I'm still not in. Can you buzz the door again?" I asked.

Over the scratchy speaker, she cleared her throat. "Hi, Orla."

"Hi."

I waited. Nothing happened.

Shit. Why hadn't I just gone over to Jenni's house instead of having to interact with Tawny? Actually, I knew why. Jenni was obsessed—and I mean really obsessed— with her upcoming wedding, and I had no doubt I'd be nothing but in the way. Last I'd seen, her house was awash in lace and tulle, and piled high with gifts shipped from all over the world. There was absolutely nothing else she was capable of talking about at that moment in time, and the last thing she needed was to hear about my bellyache of a problem.

That was beside the fact that I was far too humil-iated to let her know I'd been taken away—from the gallery my father owned—in handcuffs, all because my crazy stepsister had concluded, without even talking to me, that I was a freaking criminal.

For Christ's sake. I was a kindergarten teacher. How much more innocuous can a person get?

"Tawny, let me in goddammit," I said.

I was out of patience. I was out of fucks to give. If I had to, I'd break a window to get into my father's house.

Speaking of whom, wait until he found out what his darling little stepdaughter was up to in his absence.

After a pause, she finally responded. "Orla. Now, you know I love you. And sometimes good people do bad things. I'll never hold this against you, sweetie, but my lawyer told me not to talk to you."

Her lawyer? Why did she have a freaking lawyer?

"Okay, Tawn, don't talk to me. But just buzz me in the freaking house."

After a moment, she sighed. "Orla, that's just the problem. You can't come in the house."

"*WHAT*?" I screeched.

"Sorry, honey, but I have to go now—"

"What the fuck, Tawny?" I yelled. "This is my father's house. You wouldn't even be here if your mother hadn't snagged his stupid ass and marched him down the aisle for the umpteenth time."

Something I'd advised against, but my dad was a marrying man, and marrying was one of the things he did best.

Choosing brides, he didn't do so well. But that was on him.

"Look, where am I supposed to go, Tawny? I fucking live here."

There was no controlling it now. I was pissed.

"Look, Orla. You should have thought of that before you broke the law—"

"BUT I DIDN'T BREAK THE LAW!"

"Sorry, hon. Kiss, kiss."

And the intercom went dead.

Well fuck me sideways. I'd just been locked out of my house—well, my father's house—by some ne'er do well upstart who lucked into my family because her mother saw a good cash cow in my dumb, unsuspecting father.

Wait till he got wind of this. Problem was, however, I was pretty sure that wouldn't be for another week or two, at least according to the post card they'd sent from some remote place in Africa where they went to see a rare species of bird. Or something like that.

So, instead of breaking a window to get in, I decided to exercise my adulting skills. I drove to a local hotel.

"How long will you be staying, Miss," the front desk clerk said when I gave her my credit card and ID.

Good question.

"Let's start with… two nights, please."

Better to play it safe.

She nodded and as she ran my card, her pleasant expression turned into concern. "I'm so sorry Miss, but your card was declined. Would you like to try another?"

Oh. Right. My credit card was maxed out. So I handed her my *debit* card.

Only that one came right back, as well.

"I… I'm sorry but this card was denied, too," she said with more pity than I'd ever seen anyone muster.

"Huh. Really?"

I was tapping my card on the counter when it came back to me.

I'd emptied out my checking account bailing myself out of jail. So, both my credit *and* debit cards were useless. And I had all of twenty-eight dollars in my wallet.

Jesus fucking Christ.

Frustration exploded through me, and I ran out before I morphed into a female version of The Incredible Hulk, pissed off and mad at the world and ready to destroy anyone and anything in my path.

I got in my car and drove to a dark corner of the hotel parking lot where no one could see me, and screamed and pounded my hands on the steering wheel until I was exhausted and out of tears.

My options for finding a place to spend the night included breaking into my father's house, which would probably get me arrested *again*, or calling my BFF Jenni, who in her pre-wedding bliss would never understand how my life had become such a shit show.

So I dialed Bennie, my lawyer friend who now knew more about my sex life than he'd ever wanted to.

"Mr. Benton's office," the answering service said.

"Hi. I need to get in touch with Bennie. ASAP. He didn't respond to my text message. This is an emergency."

He'd know what to do.

After a few minutes of going round and round convincing the woman that I really did need to speak to Bennie and that I wasn't some crazy stalker, she broke the news that he was on a flight to Paris for some sort of law conference.

She could try and have him call me the next day *if he has time.*

If he has time, my ass.

I was done. *So* done.

I popped into a McDonald's drive through and comfort-stuffed my face with a Big Mac, fries, and three apple pies, splattering crumbs all over my car. Drenched in the smell of French fries and the sensation of unhealthy food sliming through my digestive system, I leaned my seat back and turned on some quiet music.

For the first time that day, even though I was essentially homeless, I closed my eyes and forced myself to relax.

But not for long.

A loud *rap* on the car window scared the shit out of me. I bolted up to see a kid in a McDonald's uniform peering down on me.

"Ma'am. You can't sleep here," he shouted as if sound didn't carry through car windows.

I waved him off and sat up in my seat, groggy from momentarily nodding off. I started the car and made a beeline out of the lot, since the burger flipper was standing there, hands on hips, making sure I vacated his otherwise empty parking lot.

I screeched into traffic, narrowly missing a late model Mercedes whose driver leaned on the horn until I was out of earshot.

And realized I had only one option left.

7

WEST 'WES' LANGLEY

My most recent case had not been one of my favorites.

I mean, we investigated cheating spouses all the time. It was the backbone of our business, and probably every other detective firm out there. Cheaters had no idea how they were providing job security for guys like me.

But the guy we were investigating now, a serial cheater who, unknown to his poor wife, had several women in the wings, liked to take his dates to the local park.

After dark.

In the bushes.

And I was the one who got to take photos with the firm's super-powered telephoto lens.

Yup. I was lately snapping shots of cheater guy fucking women in the woods where he thought he could get away with whatever he wanted.

I mean, it was one thing to tail someone and photograph them doing all sorts of things. I did that all the time. Almost every day, truth be told.

But to photograph people fucking like rabbits in the woods?

Just, no.

One of my buddies had asked if it was hot. It might have been, with different people. But not this dude and the women he brought around.

I was desperate to close this case out but my partner in it, Apollo, wanted to wait for a few more days of evidence. And he was right to lobby for that approach. I tended to be impatient, always wanting to turn my attention to something new and shiny.

Apollo was more methodical. He liked to take his time. He was a *cross all the T's and dot all the I's* kind of guy. That's why we made a good team, with Tige in the lead.

But as I pulled into the parking lot at the agency office, my thoughts were filled with what it would be like to tell the woman who'd hired us—the wife—

what her husband had been up to. I'd done it a dozen times, told people their spouses were stepping out on them. It was never easy. Usually, the people who came to us had a good idea of what was going on. And the news we shared was the final stomp on their breaking hearts that left them shattered, angry, or both.

It was days like this that I wondered if I had the stomach for this work. And I'd seen and done a lot of shit in my life.

So when I saw a strange car on the far side of our office parking lot, I felt the old familiar pricking run up the back of my neck. In my business, you never knew when some nutcase was going to lose his—or her—mind, and blame us detectives for their problems.

Of course, I was extra vigilant about these things, given my, shall we say, colorful background.

Yeah, I'd been a punk when I was a kid. Got into all sorts of trouble. And when you lived like that, you spent every day looking over your shoulder to see who was coming for you. And while I hadn't been involved in anything unsavory in years, the scanning of parking lots when I arrived pretty much anywhere was just something that would never leave my DNA. It was like all the gang beatings I'd received—and given—had ground a heightened awareness of the world into my psyche. It had been the only way to survive. Still was the only way if you asked me.

An unfamiliar car in our lot might not even register for Apollo and Tige. They'd likely think nothing of it. But I was not as easy going. I'd spent so much of my life waiting for someone or something to come get me, that I'd resigned myself to a wariness that would never go away.

I parked in my usual spot and slowly exited my car, an eye on the unfamiliar vehicle.

It seemed to be empty.

Had it been stolen? An office complex parking lot was a good place to dump a car.

I approached it slowly, doing my best to stay out of view of any mirrors, just to be safe. Once I could see inside, I saw there was a purse on the front seat, and a blanket thrown across the back.

In the shape of a human.

Fuck me. Had someone dumped a dead body? Jesus, that was going to make a mess out of our day. The cops would have to come, which was not a problem, but they'd want to ask us a million questions, and want to know a fuck load about our clients—which was confidential information we couldn't share.

I could see it now. An officer would be all up in

Tige's face, since he was the firm's principle, and they'd go round and round with questions and the non-answers everyone knew they were going to get until they tired and left.

Preferably after removing the crime scene tape they were sure to drape all over the fucking place.

That's not what we called *good for business*.

But when the lump under the blanket shifted, my pulse double-timed. Definitely not a dead body. No, whoever or whatever was under it turned over and stretched, and a small foot with bright red toenails poked out, quickly folding up again to hide from the morning chill.

Jesus. Who the fuck *was* that?

"Hello," I called, rapping my knuckles on the window.

The form beneath the blanket shifted again, and a tumble of blonde curls exploded from under it.

But that was all I could see.

"Hello," I called more loudly, checking to see if the car door was locked.

Then, the body bolted upright, and I realized the blonde hair and red toenails belonged to a young woman who'd just woken from a deep sleep.

Who thought she could camp out in our parking lot.

Yawning, she turned to face me with the groggy

eyes of a crappy night's sleep and screamed, pulling the blanket up to her chest as if she were wearing nightclothes rather than a wrinkled white blouse with the collar half-standing. Her eyes widened as we recognized each other and realized there was no threat of foul play on either end.

The woman in the car was our *new client*. The one who'd been at the office the day before with Bennie, the lawyer who often brought us clients.

Orla-something, was her name. The one Tige had apparently fucked in a seemingly-innocent one-nighter. You never know where your dick will get you, I liked to say.

I preferred my one-nighters at least in the next town over, and if possible, even farther. It was just too risky, otherwise.

This was a strange case, at least for us, Orla having been arrested for art forgery, whatever that was. What made it all the more sordid was that charges had been brought by her stepsister. And Orla's dad supposedly owned the gallery where it all went down. Problem was, there was no getting in touch with him because he was camping out some-where in freaking Africa.

On a goddamn safari.

This was some serious rich people drama.

I knew she was our client and all, but it was seriously like a car accident I couldn't look away from.

And now the woman was sleeping in our fucking parking lot.

The window on the back passenger seat rolled down and Orla stretched her neck toward the opening.

"Good morning," she chirped.

How did someone chirp after spending the night sleeping in a car?

"You're Wes, right?" she asked with a smile.

You can't make this shit up.

8

WEST 'WES' LANGLEY

"WELL. HERE I AM AGAIN."

Orla pulled her trench coat around her and looked around the office, where she'd been only the day before.

While she was nothing short of a mess, she was a cute goddamn mess with her blonde curls sticking up in different directions, a smudge of something black under her eyes, and one earring missing. She clapped her hand over her mouth and yawned again, then took the cup of coffee I offered her.

"The, um, shower is that way. Make yourself at home."

She took a sip of her coffee and winced.

It was lousy coffee on the best day, but when you were accustomed to the high-end stuff I guessed she was, well ours was a downright insult.

But I didn't give a shit and drank it all day long.

"You guys have a shower here? Cool," she said, continuing to check the place out.

When Tige took over for his dad, apparently the place hadn't been updated in years. So while we were in a pretty much boring-ass office park, Tige made the effort to renovate so we at least looked like we were in the current century. He'd done a great job. I never thought I'd work in a place this nice.

But then I didn't think I'd live to see my thirtieth birthday, either. Life was full of surprises. And I couldn't wait to see how Apollo and Tige reacted when they found out Orla had used our parking lot as her own personal campground.

"There are a couple towels in there. But I'm afraid I don't have a toothbrush or anything for you."

She gave me a little smile and patted her handbag. "Oh, that's okay. I got a toothbrush and some other stuff last night before I... well, you know... came here."

Turning on her heel, she hustled down the hall before I could ask any of the dozen questions swimming around in my head.

"Hey. Good morning," Tige said, closely followed by Apollo.

"Morning."

Tige narrowed his eyes and gestured toward the bathroom with his chin. "Why does it sound like someone is in the shower?"

Equally concerned, Apollo looked between the two of us and the bathroom door and put his hands on his hips.

I propped my ass on the corner of my desk. "Well guys, it sounds like someone's in the shower because someone *is*."

Tige frowned. "Didn't know we'd become a YMCA."

I shook my head. "Neither did I. But when I arrived this morning, that strange car out there was already in the lot. I found someone sleeping in it." I pointed out the window.

"Someone was sleeping in our lot? And now you have them in our shower?" Apollo looked at me like I'd lost my mind.

"Never fear guys. I haven't opened up our office to the local homeless community."

Actually, maybe she *was* homeless. Why else would she have slept in her car?

"So, are you gonna tell us who it is?" Tige sniped.

Of course. I was just savoring the moment. "I am.

It's Orla. Our newest client. The one from yesterday."

Two sets of eyeballs bulged.

"Orla Fellowes? No fucking way," Tige said. "You found her sleeping in that car out there?"

Fellowes. That was her family name.

"Can you believe it?" I said, shaking my head.

And just as I suspected, Apollo was concerned. Tige was bent out of shape.

"Cripes, I wonder what happened that she came here to sleep?" Apollo said. "Did she tell you anything? Is she okay?"

But before I could say a word, Tige put up his hands. "Wait, wait, wait. It's fucked up enough that she slept in her car, *here*—if you remember I was at her house the other night, and it was quite nice. What the hell happened to that place?"

"Your guess is as good as mine," I said.

He placed his fingers on his temples like he was trying to fend off one of his frequent headaches. "And then you offered her our *shower*?"

I didn't know what was more annoying to Tige— that she was using our shower or that she'd slept in our parking lot.

Or that she'd kicked him out the morning after having hooked up, and that everyone knew about it.

Or… that he'd missed out on his vacation.

When I looked at things from his perspective, I could see why he was so irritable.

"What could I do? She looked like… well, she looked like she'd spent the night sleeping in a car. I wasn't going to tell her to hit the road. She's our freaking client."

Tige laughed. "Yeah, like you would have offered her our shower if she hadn't been so good-looking."

"Hey now, Wes was just trying to help someone," Apollo said.

I settled in at my desk. I had a shitload of work to do before I left for the day to photograph people fucking in the bushes. "Whatever, guys. She'll be out in a few minutes, I'm sure. We can ask her all our questions then."

Everyone finally shut up and got to work—or pretended to—glancing up every sixty seconds to see if our guest was making her appearance.

I couldn't blame them. Orla was a stunner with that crazy, wild, long blonde hair and deep brown eyes. I'd think a woman from her background would go for a tamer, more tidy hairstyle. I liked that she let it go.

She might just have a nice little freak flag under that wrinkled trench coat.

Not that I would ever find out. Women like that didn't go for guys like me. It made total sense she'd hooked up with Tige with his preppy good looks and proper manners. They were from the same world.

Me, not so much.

"Oh, look, everybody's here."

Three heads snapped up so fast I didn't know how any of us didn't get whiplash, and we turned our complete attention to Orla. There she stood like an apparition, dressed in her skirt with the blouse untucked, running a towel over her wet hair, and barefoot.

Hell if I didn't feel a little twitching in the dick department.

Everyone was silent for a moment, as if her female energy had bewitched us or something. It was just so seldom we had a woman in the office, much less one like Orla.

Actually, we'd never had a woman like Orla in the office.

And certainly not a barefoot, slightly damp one.

Apollo was the first to recover. "So how'd you like spending the night in your car, Orla?" he asked politely.

She grimaced. "Well, it sure wasn't the Four Seasons, but the cashmere blanket in my trunk helped a lot."

"You keep a cashmere blanket in the trunk of

your car?" I asked. Shit, I'd only learned what cashmere *was* a couple months ago.

Where I grew up, people didn't have cashmere shit.

"Orla, what is going on? Can you fill us in?" Tige asked, pointing toward a chair.

She distractedly finger-combed her hair. "Yeah," she sighed. "After all the shit that went down yesterday—my being arrested, then being matched up with you guys—I went home, hoping to relax with a glass of wine and wash the jail off me. But when I got there, my bitch of a stepsister wouldn't let me into my *father's* house. If you can believe that," she shrilled, waiting for each of us to express our outrage.

Damn. That was a serious shit sandwich.

"What did you do?" Apollo asked sympathetically.

She looked down at her hands. "I went to a hotel. I was too embarrassed to call my best friend. She's planning the wedding of the century so is kind of busy. I called Bennie but he apparently flew to Paris last night, so he was of no use, either. Anyway, my credit card and debit card were both denied, so... I was kinda fucked."

"And... why were your cards denied?" Tige asked.

How did an uptown girl like Orla run out of resources to the point where she had to sleep in a goddamn car? I didn't think things like that happened to people like her.

"My credit card is maxed out, and I emptied my checking account using my debit card to pay for my freaking bail." Her voice broke.

She sniffled and dabbed at her eyes with her damp shower towel, and when the tears really started to come, she jumped out of her chair and ran for the kitchen.

We guys all looked at each other, not sure whether Orla was more surprised by her current, shitty situation, or *we* were more surprised that she'd dropped into our lives. Regardless, I hated to see a woman upset, so I hustled after her.

"Hey, Orla," I said, carefully patting her on the back.

Where I came from, you didn't touch a woman you didn't know, but fuck if I knew what else to do.

And just my luck, she turned from the kitchen counter to face me, her pretty face blotchy and red, and threw her arms around me.

About a hundred sirens sounded in my head, the loudest one saying *get her off me*. But I just stood there, arms at my side, frozen stiff.

Just as quickly, she released me. Thank god. Where I was from, this kind of shit just didn't happen.

Unwritten rules, and all that.

"Oh, Wes," she wailed, "I don't know how, in a matter of twenty-four hours, my life turned into such a mess." She sniffled again and shook her head hard as if that would make it go away.

"Anyway," she sighed. "Sorry about the outburst."

She pulled on her high-heels and trench coat, which she'd left in the kitchen before her shower, and grabbed her purse.

"I'm heading down to the gallery. I need to talk to Tawny. Try to make her understand I'm not the bad guy."

Oh Christ. Pretty sure that was about the worst thing she could do at that moment.

"Um, Orla, I don't think that's a good idea—"

She blew her nose one more time, ignoring my advice. "Thanks, Wes. You've been a great help," she said and headed for the door.

I stood there in the kitchen, shaking my head over the bad decisions I saw people make day in and day out. I just didn't get it sometimes.

"Guys," I said, returning to our big shared office, "Orla just split."

Tige's head snapped up from his computer. "What? Where'd she go?"

I took a deep breath. "She… went to the gallery to talk to her stepsister."

Apollo got to his feet. "Oh shit. Not a good idea."

Tige joined him. "Jesus. Talk about jumping from the frying pan into the fire. Is she fucking crazy?"

I held my hands up. "I told her it wasn't a good idea."

Tige nodded. "Okay. Well, that means we need to get over there ASAP before she gets her ass arrested again." He grabbed his keys.

"You guys coming?" he asked.

Apollo nodded and headed for the door.

But I didn't need to answer. They knew I wouldn't miss a shitshow like this for all the money in the world.

9

ORLA FELLOWES

"THAT WOULD BE LOVELY, MR. DALT. AND I'M SO sorry about the drama when you were here yesterday. It's so hard to find honest employees."

Holy shit. Was that motherfucking stepsister of mine really on the phone with a client who *I* brought in, trash-talking *me*?

There she sat, behind the humongous glass desk *my* father had outfitted her with, like a queen on her throne. She wiggled in her skin-tight shift dress, swinging her crossed legs and bouncing the heel of her tall black pump against the plushy rug under her chair.

The nerve.

But instead of starting a war, I tip-toed past her office to mine to get my laptop and other desk stuff.

But before I even got started, there was a loud gasp behind me.

Dammit.

"WHAT ARE YOU DOING HERE?" she barked.

I didn't look up from the drawer I was emptying into my purse. There wasn't much to collect anyway, aside from lipstick and tampons and a couple Moleskine notebooks. But hell if I were going to leave anything for her to enjoy. And the laptop had been a gift from my father, so she definitely couldn't have that.

I stood to my full height and took a step toward her. She took a step back.

That's right, bitch.

"I'm getting my things since the police officers you sicced on me yesterday were in such a hurry to take me down to the station and book me. Tell me, Tawny," I said, taking another step toward her, "have you ever been arrested? Do you know what it's like?"

Her head twitched for a moment, and then her scowl returned. "No, I do not. But you wouldn't either if you hadn't broken the law."

I turned back to my desk, but she grabbed my

arm and spun me. "You can't have that stuff. Put it back," she demanded.

I dropped my bag and got in her face. "Do. Not. Touch. Me. Ever."

The ferocity I felt must have come through loud and clear because the arrogance in her eyes was colored by fear. She let go.

But I wasn't done. "You're going to pay for this, Tawny. Accusing me of some bullshit and then getting me arrested."

She scoffed. "Threaten all you want, Orla. You are going to pay for what you did. Imagine, endangering a business your father is backing. What a horrible daughter you are."

Really? Was that the best she had?

"Look," I said, shaking a finger in her face, "I still don't understand what you are accusing me of, but I will prove you're full of shit. And when I do, my father will kick you and your skank mother out of our house. Forever!" I screamed. "Just like you locked me out last night!"

I would have loved to smack the smug off her face.

"I'm sure you have no idea what you've done," she taunted. "Poor, innocent little Orla. Well, your good-girl act has come to an end. Tell me, how did you find someone to copy our most expensive paintings? And what did you do with the originals?"

"Are you kidding? I wouldn't begin to know how to do any of that shit. And you know it. So, if someone stole from our gallery, or copied paintings, or whatever, you've got the wrong person. I don't know why you'd point your finger at me anyway. I'm your freaking stepsister."

"Exactly. I can't believe *you'd* do this to *me*." She sniffed like I'd broken her heart or something.

With my meager belongings stuffed in my purse and my laptop under my arm, I attempted to walk around her to get the hell out of the place.

"I told you, you cannot take those things," she said quietly, remaining in front of me.

"Get the fuck out of my way," I growled.

Please, please give me an excuse to slug her. I didn't care if she gave me a black eye—all I needed was for her to take the first swing.

Then I could go Rambo on her skanky, skinny ass.

"I will not," she shrilled.

Fine. Shit was getting ugly.

But just when I was about to *take off my hoops*, as they say, the front doorbell jingled.

"Ladies, ladies," Tige said, whipping around the

corner to where Tawny and I were having our stand-off. "Take it down a notch, okay?"

Tawny looked him up and down, then Wes and Apollo. I could swear something passed over her face when she noticed how good-looking they were.

"And who are you?" she sang.

Tige took my arm. "C'mon, Orla. You shouldn't be here."

He was right. And since I had my stuff, I let him lead me toward the door.

But not before noticing Tawny doing a double-take. Their hot good looks would be hard for any woman to miss, much less an opportunist like my stepsister.

And like she did whenever she wanted something, she changed her tone abruptly. "Can I… can I ask who you gentlemen are?" she asked demurely.

Wes lumbered up to her—it was the only way to describe it—and pulled out a business card. Then we continued to the door.

"You are… private detectives?" she said in a choked voice.

Interesting reaction.

"Yes, they are, you shit for brains. Did you think I was going to take this sitting down? And wait till my father hears the whole story. You'll regret even getting out of bed the day you had me arrested you—"

Even though my arms were mostly full, I lunged at Tawny anyway. I knew I couldn't do anything to her, but I wanted to at least scare her for one delicious moment.

And it worked. She jumped back, then watched us exit the gallery. But before the doors closed, I screamed at her again.

"Just wait till the world finds out what a monster you are, Tawny. Just wait."

I'm sure my words did nothing to make her regret her actions, but when passersby on the sidewalk stopped and turned, I knew I'd delivered her the worst punishment I could.

Because god knew how she'd carefully cultivated her reputation in town. The last thing she wanted was to give anyone anything to gossip about.

But all that would change if I had anything to do with it.

10

ORLA FELLOWES

ONE OF THE GUYS DROVE MY CAR BACK TO THE OFFICE because, apparently, I was too 'upset' to drive myself. While I was pretty sure I could manage the two-mile distance, I didn't really mind, especially since we picked up sandwiches on our way back.

The four of us settled around the conference room table, the place I'd been when I'd realized my one-nighter was also about to become my own personal detective.

That was not my best moment.

"So, Orla," Wes said, taking a swig of his ice tea, "where are you going to crash while we're working all this out? I know you said your friend and Bennie were not options."

He hadn't missed the way I'd been trying to coax the kinks out of my neck the past couple hours from having slept poorly in my car. It was hard to be discreet about shoulder and neck rolls—not that I needed to. But it did end up drawing attention to my immediate needs.

Bonus.

And of course I'd racked my brains figuring out where I might stay, too. I hadn't slept in my car because I'd thought it would be fun, for heaven's sake. But Jenni was simply not an option, at least not right now, and all my other friends, at least the ones I kept in touch with, had moved away or not returned after college.

Dad wasn't returning for another week or so, so that ruled out his house.

I couldn't fucking believe it.

I was homeless.

"I… I think I could maybe track my dad down on his safari. The outfitter has an emergency number for getting messages to people."

I didn't want to ruin his vacation, but maybe it was time to get in touch. There was no denying things were at a new low when someone was forced to sleep in a car.

I set down my egg salad sandwich. "I never thought I'd say this, but I'm stuck. Totally, fucking stuck. It's crazy. I didn't think I'd ever be in a situation like this."

Did anybody ever think they'd end up in a situation like this?

I'd always had a slightly 'off' feeling about Tawny and her stepmother, much more so than I had about any of the other families my father had brought into our lives. Should I have known something like this might happen? Or at least suspected it?

Looking back, returning to town after the boyfriend break up and snagging the job at Tawny's gallery had all fallen into place so easily. Like freakishly easily.

That's not usually how life worked. I should have suspected something would go wrong.

I swallowed. "You... you guys could loan me some money until my father returns and helps me straighten all this crap out. It won't be too long..." My voice trailed off when I saw how enthused they were by the thought of fronting me living expenses.

"You know I'm good for it," I said hopefully.

Maybe not.

But Apollo tapped his finger against his head. "You know guys," he said, looking around, "we do need an admin."

Tige turned to me, his head tilted. "Our admin bailed on us last week when she won a casino jackpot or something. Informed us she wasn't coming back."

How nice for her.

I looked around. "So? What does that have to do with me?"

"Well," he continued, "you need the help of some detectives, and we need the help of an admin. Maybe we could work something out. We have a pull-out sofa, and that shower you used this morning, right here in the office."

They thought I might come work for them? That seemed a little crazy.

At first.

"You're saying I could work for you in exchange for, well, everything I need?" I had to laugh at that, it sounded so preposterous.

"Look. You've got nothing to lose. You have no money for a retainer for your case, and we need office help. There's no downside while you're getting back on your feet," Tige said.

Wes leaned toward me. "Look, Orla. You don't really have any other options at the moment."

Something about the reality of that hit me. Hard. I really did have no other options, did I?

Oh, how did I ever end up in such a pinch? Had I

trusted the wrong people? Made bad choices? Had I always been so cluelessly vulnerable, bumbling through life with blinders on, trusting that things would always, or nearly always, work out?

I was afraid of what the answer was.

I'd thought I was so smart leaving the dirtbag boyfriend, and moving back to my dad's to start over. But maybe this was the universe's way of saying it was my turn for a shit sandwich. Everyone gets one every now and then, and it seemed like it was just my turn.

And unless I wanted to sleep in the back seat of my car again, I'd better find out more about what the guys were offering.

11

APOLLO BECK

I COULDN'T REMEMBER THE LAST TIME I'D SEEN MY father.

But there he was, coming out of the dry cleaner's just as I'd pulled into the lot.

I grabbed my shirts from the back seat of the car with the intention of crossing the parking lot to say hello to my dad, but then thought better of it.

That morning, I had neither the time nor energy to face the man. For years now, my father had waited for the day I came to him to admit private detective work was a career mistake. That he'd been right all along that someone from my background and privilege should become a doctor or lawyer or some other high-status profession.

He was going to be waiting a long, long time.

And sad as it was, if that meant I wouldn't be talking to him, possibly forever, then so be it.

Actually, this was the case with not only my father, but my whole family. I was bred from a long line of snobs who did all they could to hang on to their perceived status, which had been once earned by an industrialist great-grandfather a hundred or so years earlier. Who, by the way, exploited child labor and committed a host of other business affronts that would never be permitted today. But the family didn't talk about those things.

One thing I knew would interest my father was that the firm was working with someone from the Fellowes family—a clan that went back in our town almost as far as my family did, wealthy financiers that they were, and popular local philanthropists.

Which made it all the more strange that the lovely Orla Fellowes had found herself in the predicament she was in.

But I'd never betray a client's privacy, so the only way Dad would find out I was working with her was if it somehow became public. Which, given the outburst between Orla and Tawny the day before, their mess wasn't going to stay private for very long.

I knew from hearing him gripe over the years that my dad had some sort of beef with Dominic Fellowes, Orla's dad. The details weren't clear—nor did I care for them to be—but the issue seemed to be around a property dispute going back decades that remained unresolved. I doubted Orla's father gave a shit that my dad walked the face of the earth still steaming over their misunderstanding, and that made my father even madder.

The insult of being ignored was far worse than the insult that kicked off the whole feud to begin with.

Funny that.

If dad were aware I was working with Orla Fellowes, well that would seriously chap his ass, but also kill him with curiosity. And that I couldn't risk. So I didn't run my shirts into the cleaners until I watched him exit the lot and be on his way.

What would further irritate him was knowing that my primary case that week, which I was working on with Wes, was investigating a man who was cheating on his wife with the wife of the mayor. And some other local women too, apparently.

To further complicate things, there was something about them having sex in the local park after dark. But Wes was dealing with that point.

Dad was, after all, friends with the mayor, and

would never approve of anything that might upset his image, even if it were his wife who was doing the stepping out.

It was all so… unseemly, as he would say.

So as far as family relations went, I was doing great stacking up multiple reasons for Dad to detest or be ashamed of me.

I'd nearly arrived at the office when I was almost T-boned by someone running a red light. I slammed on my brakes in time to avoid a terrible collision, but also in time to spill the hot coffee I'd just picked up all over the lap of my clean trousers.

Fuck me.

Great way to start the day.

Grabbing a couple napkins from my glove box, I mopped up the worst of my coffee spill, and when I got to the office, removed my trousers and headed to the kitchen to try and clean them as best I could.

That's when I heard noise coming from the back of the office.

Shit. Had we been broken into again?

Why anyone would break into our office was beyond me. There was no cash, no valuables, and we took our laptops with us every night when we left. But I guess there's always some asshole out there hoping to hit the jackpot.

But all that speculation was put to rest when our

new client and admin, Orla, walked out of the bathroom and into the kitchen.

Butt naked.

That's right. Like, wearing no clothes.

I'd forgotten she was staying there. Shit.

We stood staring at each other for several
seconds. Then, Orla turned on her heel and ran back
to the bathroom, her cute little ass cheeks jiggling
the tiniest amount.

And I stood there in my boxers, watching her.

While I'd forgotten she was there, she'd apparently forgotten that our office wasn't her private
living room. The woman was full of no end of
surprises. Who the hell knew what to expect from
her next.

"Sorry, Orla," I called as she slammed the door.
"I'll have my trousers back on in a minute. Dealing
with spilled coffee." I might have been in my dress
shirt and boxers but at least I wasn't completely
nude.

Although, my surprising the shit out of Orla, and
her freezing in place, gave me a few good seconds to
check her out.

Down boy.

So I'd seen her naked. So what? We were all
adults.

The bathroom door opened a crack. "I'm dressed now, Apollo. Let me know when I can come out."

I yanked my wet trousers back on, now cold and clinging to my crotch.

"Ready," I called.

She sheepishly made her way out, wearing the same skirt and white blouse she'd had on for the last few days, avoiding my gaze as I made coffee.

"Sorry about that," she mumbled. "I thought… oh, never mind. It doesn't matter."

I wasn't complaining.

None of us knew how long Orla would be with us, but her crashing in our office was not looking like a long-term solution. I wasn't sure it was even a short-term solution. And because the house I shared with Wes had an extra room, I wanted to propose that she crash there for the duration of her… homelessness.

But I didn't get a chance to bring it up. As she was pouring herself a cup of coffee, there was a loud crash, and there she stood, gripping the handle of her coffee mug. Only there was no mug attached to it. The two pieces had separated, the mug crashing to the floor, splattering coffee everywhere.

For a moment, I wanted to laugh. Orla looked so pitiful standing there holding onto the mug handle for dear life, while the mess at her feet spread.

Instead of laughing though, I grabbed the roll of paper towels I'd been using to clean my trousers, and crouched to help her clean the mess.

As she picked up shards of the broken mug, I noticed her shoulders begin to shake, followed by a stifled sob.

I didn't blame her for being upset. Not a lot of things had been going right for her. Shit, I'd probably cry, too, if I were her.

So I took her by the elbows and helped her stand, taking the broken pieces of mug from her and tossing them in the trash. When I led her to a chair to sit down, she actually stumbled.

What a mess.

"I'm sorry, Orla. I'm sorry things have been so fucked up for you," I said. And I meant it. She seemed like a cool woman who was hopefully just running through a spell of bad luck.

I pulled her into my arms as her face crumpled. She fell into me, crying quietly, turning her head on occasion to blow her nose. This pushed her hair into my face, which I couldn't help but notice smelled amazing. Fresh and clean, thanks to the shower in our office.

And damn if she didn't feel great in my arms. I'd been on a serious woman dry spell, and it had been ages since I'd held a beautiful one.

Actually, I'd probably never held a woman as beautiful as Orla.

Who now worked for me, as I worked for her. How the hell did that crazy arrangement happen?

"You… you gonna be okay, Orla?" I asked, half hoping she'd hang on to me for a while longer.

She let out a long sigh. "Mmmm hmmm," she murmured as she turned her face up to mine.

And like it was the most natural thing in the world, I lowered my lips to hers and tasted the woman I'd been thinking about non-stop since the day she'd turned up in our offices.

"Um. Excuse me."

We both turned to the doorway, where Wes stood, his face covered in a smirk, watching us like we were two bad children.

"Oh. Morning, Wes," I said, leisurely releasing Orla.

We were already busted, so there was no point in pretending nothing had happened.

"Morning, Apollo. Orla," he said, continuing to smirk. "Hey, when you guys get a chance, you know, when you're not so *busy*, let's sit down and discuss our latest infidelity case. I have an idea about how Orla might be able to help."

The one involving the mayor's wife. Just thinking about it gave me indigestion.

Orla's eyebrows rose. "Okay. I'll have time in just a moment," she said, heading back to the mess we'd been cleaning up.

Wes nodded. "Cool. Give me a holler."

Five minutes later, we were in the conference room where we'd first met Orla. I wasn't surprised she took a seat at the end of the table, avoiding my gaze at all costs, focusing instead on Wes, with a strange intensity. I probably shouldn't have kissed her, especially if she were going to end up so damn embarrassed about it, even if she had launched herself into my arms.

Dumb-ass move on my part.

"Glad you guys could fit me in," Wes teased.

Because he could.

Orla turned bright pink. I scowled at him so he'd back off. I could take his ribbing, but Orla was new to it. No need to make her feel like kissing me was the worst of it.

Unless it was.

"What's your idea Wes? I'm all ears," I said.

He interlaced his fingers on the table, and leaned toward us like he was making some kind of great offer.

"As you know, we are tailing… shall we call him Mr. Doe? I haven't been able to get any great shots of him in the woods with his—"

"*What?*" Orla exclaimed. "This guy is doing… stuff in the woods?"

She looked like she might vomit. Guess she'd never had sex outdoors.

"Yes, Orla. He takes his conquests to the downtown park after dark and they… you know."

She pressed her lips together, then burst out laughing. "Oh my god. You have to photograph stuff like *that?*"

Wes didn't find it funny. He'd made clear his distaste for the project from the get-go. But hey, that was our job. "Unfortunately, Orla, yes. I photograph people fucking in the bushes. When necessary."

He tossed his pen on the conference room table and sat back in his seat, still bitter about that part of his job description.

At Wes's show of dissatisfaction, Orla wiped the smile off her face. "Tell me how I can help, Wes."

He took a deep breath. "What I propose, Orla, is that you serve as bait."

Bait? No. No way.

"Geez. How… how would that work?" she asked in a small voice, glancing nervously between the two of us.

"We'll get you all dressed up and plant you someplace we know Mr. Doe frequents. He'll likely hit on you, we'll get some photos, and be done with it. Easy."

It was never that easy. I knew that. He knew that. Orla didn't.

She nodded slowly. "Sounds... simple enough. I've never done anything like that, though. Actually, I'd never done a lot of things that I've done this week. First times and all that..."

She gave a weak laugh and her eyes filled with tears again.

I would have reached out to pat her arm or something if she hadn't sat so far away from me like I had cooties. For cripes sake, she was still trying not to look at me any more than she had to.

Wes cleared his throat. I didn't take him for the kind of guy who was comfortable with female emotion, and it was looking like I was right.

But the bottom line was, his plan just might work. We could frame Mr. Doe doing his worst, and move on, saving the mayor as much humiliation as possible.

And hopefully not push Orla over the edge she was so precipitously close to.

🔍

12

ORLA FELLOWES

Barely twenty-four hours ago I was a gallery assistant living at my dad's super-nice house, having left behind a loser ex and my kindergarten teaching job, and was planning on helping my BFF Jenni plan her over-the-top wedding. Not a bad set-up.

How quickly that had disintegrated.

I'd been arrested.

Locked out of my home.

Slept in my car.

Worn the same clothes for three days straight.

Moved into an office where I slept on a pull-out couch.

Been avoiding my BFF due to embarrassment.

And been seen naked by a private detective I was supposedly working for, whom I'd also kissed passionately because he was so fucking good-looking.

Who smelled nice, too.

Now, I was going to be 'bait,' whatever the hell that meant, for a crazy plan of Wes's that would help the guys trap some dirty dog who'd been stepping out on his wife.

And why the hell not? There wasn't anything normal about my life anymore. Might as well just pile on more weird shit.

"I'll do it. Sounds interesting."

Not. But I hated cheaters. In a sick way, it would be good to fuck one up.

Besides, I worked for the guys now, and god knew they'd been good to me. I wasn't in a position to say no when they needed me for something. As long as it was lawful.

Speaking of which. "Hey. This isn't illegal, is it?" I asked.

Apollo tapped the table. "Excellent question. If the police were doing it, it could be considered entrapment. But the advantage of working with private detectives is that we aren't bound by the same rules."

Oh. Goody.

Joining us, Tige grabbed a seat.

"Morning," I said.

He nodded in my direction. "Apollo is right. It's not entrapment. If Mr. Doe approached a woman sitting there pretending to mind her own business, that's one thing. But if a woman approached Mr. Doe by throwing herself all over him to set him up, that could be considered coercive, and therefore entrapment. So, there's a fine line."

Maybe this shit wasn't for me.

He ran his fingers through his neatly styled hair, roughing it up a bit. He was cute and nice and I'd been feeling shitty for saying he wasn't that great in bed. It wasn't true. He was actually freaking awesome. I'd just been mad that day.

"That's how my dad always ran it, and it worked for him for fifty years," he added.

Wes slapped his hand on the table. "Great. This is good stuff. We'll see how Mr. Doe reacts and hopefully wrap things up."

"What about the mayor?" Apollo asked.

The mayor? What about the mayor?

Tige and Wes shot him a dirty look and said nothing, then avoided looking at me.

Okay. Fine. I'm not supposed to know anything

about the mayor. Except that my father couldn't stand him.

"My dad says the mayor is an asshole."

Now everyone was looking at me.

"What? Isn't that common knowledge? He got elected because of his money or something?" I added.

Tige laughed. "Well, Apollo's dad doesn't think the mayor's an asshole."

"He doesn't?" I asked.

Apollo laughed. "My dad knows the mayor. They're friends. He knows your father, too."

Huh?

"Your dad knows my dad? Really?" I asked.

Apollo nodded slowly. "I think they had business dealings a long time ago or something."

"Oh. Funny. And here we are, sort-of working together," I laughed.

But Apollo didn't laugh. Did he know something I didn't?

Wes quickly changed the subject. "So, guys, if Orla is going to go undercover for us, we need to get her some clothes."

I waved his concern away. "Oh, don't worry Wes. I've got tons of clothes at home—"

They looked at me in surprise.

Oh. Right. "My clothes at *home*. The *home* I can't get into."

I felt that damn lump growing in my throat again. But I was tired of crying. Tired of feeling sorry for myself. And tired of bellyaching about whether I'd made good decisions or bad. Shit had happened that was out of my control, and I was doing my best to come back from it. All things considered, I was pretty fucking lucky.

Lucky I had enough money to pay for bail.

Lucky Bennie had introduced me to the guys.

And lucky, actually, that Tawny had shown her true colors. She was so going to pay for shit when I was done with her. It was just a matter of time. And I was patient.

"We'll get you some money out of petty cash. That okay?" Tige asked.

Cash? For shopping? Of course that was okay. Actually, it was more than okay. It was freaking awesome. A little retail therapy would be the perfect pick-me-up.

Tige left the room and came back with a wad of cash. "Here's five hundred dollars. Do you think that will be enough?"

FIVE HUNDRED DOLLARS?

"Oh, um, sure, that will be fine. Thank you." I took a deep breath to steady my voice and stuffed it in my purse. "Now can you give me an idea of what you'd like me to get? I've never been bait before."

I laughed nervously.

Wes shrugged. "You know. Something... attractive. I mean... you know what guys like, don't you?"

I suppose I did. "Something low cut? High slit? Stiletto heels?"

I knew what I thought would attract a guy, but that didn't mean it was what the guys had in mind. "Would you... would one of you come shopping with me? Just to make sure I got the right stuff?"

Apollo quickly volunteered. "Sure, I have some time today."

"Perfect," I said, popping to my feet. "Let's head out after lunch. I know a couple shops that will be perfect."

Several hours later, I emerged from a dressing room wearing a slinky wrap dress. The way it crossed over my chest showcased a little cleavage—not so much to be tacky, but enough to be alluring—and when I walked, the skirt flipped open, revealing a respectable amount of thigh.

I must have chosen well, because when I did a little spin for Apollo, his mouth dropped open.

"Holy shit," he mumbled, looking me up and down.

Crap. Had I gone too far? Red faced, I headed back into the dressing room. It didn't seem right to be all sexy in front of someone I was working for.

Even if I had already kissed him.

"Orla, hold up. Sorry. I didn't mean to gawk. It's just that… that red dress is breathtaking on you."

My heart thudded in my chest at the sort of compliment one didn't get every day, and the growing heat on my face told me that if I didn't get my shit under control, I'd soon be as red as the dress.

"Oh. Well, thanks. That's nice of you to say." I continued to the dressing room.

But Apollo gently took my arm before I could walk away. "Hold on. Hold on, Orla," he said.

"Yeah?"

"Don't be embarrassed. You are a beautiful woman. I know this feels weird, to be dressing up to attract someone you don't know and probably don't want to know. But it's a huge help to us, and to the client. We appreciate it."

I looked at his hand, still holding my arm. "That makes me feel better. Helps reduce some of the creep factor."

Keep the eye on the ball and all that.

"And Orla, don't worry. I'll be right there. You'll be safe."

I wasn't so sure that having Apollo close by was what I would call 'safe,' given our kiss of earlier. But I was willing to give it a try.

13

ORLA FELLOWES

"What will you have, miss?"

I glanced at the backlit bottles of clear and amber liquor on the wall behind the bar, then back at the smiling bartender.

I think I'll have a club soda."

As tempting as it was to get something stronger, I wasn't about to risk being at my sharpest. The guys had promised this would be a quick and easy assignment, but I was new to the role of 'bait,' and while it wasn't something I'd ever thought I'd be doing, I figured I might as well do the best job I could.

Might look nice on a resume at some point.

In order that I didn't fall out of my wrap dress, I kept my back ramrod straight, but every time I tried to seductively cross my legs, I smashed my knee on the bar.

Earning some nice shiners for later.

As I sipped my bubbly water, the sleeve of an expensive suit jacket brushed against my wrist. In my nervousness, I jerked away, but when I realized it was just Apollo, I giggled.

Like an idiot.

"Don't look at me," he said quietly.

I quickly diverted my attention back to the bubbles in my soda. "Sorry," I whispered.

Apollo waved the bartender over and ordered himself a Macallan whiskey, throwing a hundred-dollar bill down on the bar.

Damn, this man knew how to roll.

"I came over to tell you to relax. He'll be along. Be patient. He comes here for a drink on his way home from work every night, so stop fidgeting. You are absolutely gorgeous, and I am here to keep things moving forward. Just try to be natural. You know?"

Well, shit. Good thing it was dark in the bar because I knew my face turned a couple shades of pink.

And even though I wasn't supposed to, I glanced in his direction and started to say *thank you*, but he was already gone. I was dying to turn and see where he'd disappeared to, but remembered he'd told me to play it cool.

After a couple deep breaths, I leaned back in my barstool to get my chill on, and took a casual look around the bar. There were a couple men seated at a two-top nearby. One of them tilted his head and raised his glass to me. I returned a small smile.

It was interesting. I wasn't used to this kind of attention. It wasn't that I was usually ignored by men, but I just didn't put myself in a situation where I was at a bar, alone, dressed to the nines.

The guys were right. Men noticed this shit.

"Excuse me, bartender. I'll have a scotch," a deep voice said from a couple bar stools away.

Shit. Was that him?

The guys had shown me some photos, but I didn't want to look just yet.

Turned out I didn't have to wait long to get my look. Within five minutes he'd helped himself to the seat right next to me, so raring to go I could feel the heat emanating off his body.

I could also smell the mint he must have just popped into his mouth.

And the cologne he must have just sprayed on god knew what body part.

"You have amazing hair," he said, leaning toward me.

Not the best opening line, but not the worst, either.

I glanced at him shyly. Yup, that was him all right. "Thanks," I murmured.

"What's your name?" he asked.

Shit. Should I give my real name?

"O—Ophelia."

I looked back up at him and could see why women liked him. He was probably forty-ish with a little gray at the temples and sparkly blue eyes. Strong jaw and perfect teeth.

Jerk.

He glanced down at my cleavage, then at my lips, then back to my eyes. He was skilled. I had to hand him that.

"Ophelia. Guess your parents were Hamlet fans?" he asked, swiveling to face me on his barstool.

Remembering why I was there, I turned slightly toward him, glancing through the bar to see where Apollo was and if he was getting the photos he needed.

I didn't see him anywhere.

"Yes, they were. Are you a Hamlet fan?" I asked.

One corner of his mouth turned up in a half-smile. "No. But I am an Ophelia fan."

Queue the cheese. It was amazing what women fell for.

But I wasn't there to be judgmental.

"That's a good one. And what is your name?" I asked.

He extended his hand. "Don. Don Johnson."

I had to look away at that one to keep from bursting out laughing. If I hadn't been on the job, I might have suggested he try something more original. Or interesting.

But shit, it seemed to get him laid, so what did I know?

Next I knew, his hand was on my knee. I glanced down in alarm but took a deep breath. This was how it was supposed to be happening, right?

And once again, I looked around the bar for signs of Apollo. Nothing.

That's when I realized we hadn't discussed what I'd call an exit strategy. How long was I to sit around with Don Johnson? Would I know when the time was right to get the hell out of there?

Shit, shit, shit.

But when his hand slid up my dress to my mid-thigh, I'd had enough. If Apollo didn't have the photos he needed, it was too fucking bad. I waved the bartender over to pay for my club soda.

"Oh here, let me get that," Don Johnson said,

throwing some cash down on the bar. "You heading out?"

Getting to my feet, I nodded. "Yeah. Gotta get home… to my baby."

His gaze shot to my hands. "I don't see any wedding rings on those fingers," he crooned.

Think fast.

"Right. Good observation. Now, I'll be heading out… Don."

So he jumped down from his bar stool, too, and followed me. "Let me walk you to your car, Ophelia."

I picked up my pace. "That's not necessary, but thanks anyway."

He wasn't giving up. "You know, Ophelia, beautiful women like you shouldn't walk alone after dark. It's not wise."

I looked up at him when I reached my car, but didn't unlock the doors. I had no idea where Apollo was, nor what this man might do. Thank god I'd parked under a street lamp

"Say, my car is just a couple blocks away. Can I ask you to give me a lift?" he asked.

I didn't care if his car was on the moon. I wasn't going anywhere with him. "Sorry, Don. Can't help you with that."

Still not deterred, he leaned toward me until I was pressed back against my car. He put one hand on either side of me, effectively blocking me from moving, and lowered his face to mine.

I shoved both my hands against his chest, but he didn't budge.

So I yelled. "Back off!"

"C'mon Ophelia," he said when I turned my face away from his.

And suddenly I was free.

I watched him violently pulled away from me, wearing a look of surprise I wish I could have caught on camera.

Apollo had him around the neck, dragging him until he lost his footing and splattered to the ground. "The lady told you to back the fuck off!" Apollo yelled, pinning him with a hard shoe on the chest. That was going to leave quite a footprint on this white dress shirt.

While Don Johnson tried unsuccessfully to get out from under Apollo, I jumped in my car and sped away, ready to just go back to the loser ex if it meant *this* part of my life would go away.

Just go away, as if it never happened.

14

TIGE ST. JAMES

WELL, SHIT.

We'd gotten all the evidence we needed for Mr. Doe, but at what cost? Orla returned to the office just as Wes and I were leaving, shaking as if she'd just come in from the cold.

Except that it was a warm evening.

"Orla, how'd it go? And where is Apollo?" Wes called over his shoulder, already going through the evidence photos Apollo had emailed him.

I hoped our client was going to be satisfied. The guy who tried to force himself on Orla was in jail and wouldn't be hitting on any more women for a while.

Thank god.

Orla plopped down on the sofa and stared like she was catatonic.

Fuck. What had happened?

I took a seat next to her and grabbed her hands, warming them up between my own.

My reaction surprised me, but I was overcome with a sudden urge to protect her. She'd faced a lot lately, and we guys wanted to help her—not set her back.

Which I was afraid we might have just done.

So bizarre to go from a meaningless one-nighter to where we were now. But getting to know her better had actually been kind of cool. Even if I'd had to put off my kayaking vacation.

Thinking back, I hadn't intended for our hook-up to be a one-off. I'd actually really enjoyed her that night, even before we'd gotten to her bedroom. In fact, I'd been thinking about it nearly every night since.

But sitting there on the sofa in my office that evening, she didn't even notice my touch. Staring into the distance, she tapped her shoes on the floor and stared ahead.

Wes finally noticed something was up. "Orla? What's going on?"

I threw an arm around her shoulder and pulled her to me when she didn't respond. "C'mon, Orla. We're taking you home. You're not staying here tonight."

Finally, she sighed. "Okay," she said in a flat voice, letting me pull her to her feet.

Wes wrapped Orla's trench around her and flicked off the lights while I locked up. "Honey, did something happen we need to know about? Because if anyone hurt you, I will destroy that motherfucker—"

Wes and I caught each other's gaze.

Fuck me. What was happening to us? It seemed the lovely Orla Fellowes was getting under our skin.

In a good way.

And I could see why. I mean, in the face of the shit storm that was her life in recent days, she still managed to be chipper and upbeat. Even funny from time to time.

We guys had similar tastes in women—that was nothing new. We all dug a smart, funny, and of course good-looking woman who took no shit. Or tried not to take shit.

She finally shook off whatever was making her catatonic. "The guy—Mr. Doe—got kind of aggressive out by my car. I hadn't expected it. Apollo pulled him off me, and I split. I don't know how I could have been so naïve, but I hadn't expected anything like that."

She shook her head as Wes and I walked her out to our car.

When we got her home, we took her to the guest room and I ran a hot bath for her. I didn't know what else to do, but remembered my mother would do that for herself after a long day. I even squeezed some hotel bath bubbles I found under the sink.

"I'll check back in ten minutes, but holler if you need anything," I said.

I joined Wes in the kitchen, where he sat with his head in his hands. "Holy shit. I guess that was a big fucking mistake on my part, asking her to pose as bait."

I patted him on the back. "Lesson learned for all of us. But don't beat yourself up, man. None of us knew Mr. Doe was predatory in addition to being a cheating husband. Apollo will be home in a bit to fill us in on the details."

He stood. "I'm bringing Orla some tea."

When I was alone in the kitchen, I had a moment to think for myself. There were so many things we could have done differently, not least of which was making sure our 'bait' had some self-defense skills.

Fuck, I felt like shit.

And just when I thought I couldn't beat myself up any more than I had, I heard a soft giggle come from the back of the house—where the guest room was.

Was Orla snapping out of her funk?

And why was I obsessing so badly over her?

She was a freaking client. And an employee.

And someone I'd had a one-nighter with.

When I heard another soft laugh followed by Wes's rough guffaw, the tension in my shoulders began to dissipate. And my curiosity began to grow.

I walked toward the sound, making as much noise as possible on the hardwood floors so they'd hear me coming, and when I got to the door, which was hanging wide open, Orla was standing there wrapped in a bath towel. She was about half the size of the gigantic Wes, and he was trying to run a comb through her wet hair.

Wes combing a woman's hair. Now that was something I never thought I'd see from the bald, pierced, and tattooed former gang member. But the truth of it was, I knew he was a gentle giant. His care for Orla made sense.

Wes glanced over his shoulder. "Hey, dude. Come on in. Let's see if you're any better at dealing with this rat's nest than I am."

Orla turned to look at me, the nipples on her little tits protruding through her towel.

I was pretty sure I was going to be worse than fucking useless trying to comb Orla's hair, but I'd been dying to touch her again since the night we'd had together—even though she'd indicated I wasn't too talented in the nooky department. Regardless, I damn well wasn't turning down an opportunity now. I took the comb from Wes's hand, and stuck it into her tangles.

"Ouch!" she said, laughing, as Wes moved around to her front.

Without hesitation, he dropped to his knees, and with his hands on her tits, lifted her towel and drove his tongue between her legs.

Dude didn't waste any time.

I threw the comb aside as her head dropped back onto my chest, her eyes fluttering closed and her mouth turning into a pretty little 'O.' And with a little nudge, her towel fell to the floor.

Oops.

And my dick was now at full-mast.

Wes looked up at me. "Fucking delicious. You want some, Tige?"

Holding Orla's head, I ran my lips down the side of her neck. "If it's okay with our beautiful girl."

Her eyes popped open. "Yes, please," she said.

Well, well. Our girl had kicked ass and come back stronger for it.

By the time I'd adjusted my painful erection and knelt before the beautiful Orla, Wes already had his cock out and in her hand.

That guy was a serious baller. He just kept things moving right along.

I could smell Orla's excitement even before I got close to it, and it was the most fucking sweet thing I'd ever smelled. And when I touched her little clit with my starving tongue, she pushed lightly into my face for more.

Just like she had the night we'd spent together.

"Goddamn, baby," I murmured, my tongue diving between her puffy lips.

I parted her legs by placing one foot up on the bed, and ran my fingers through her wet excitement, stopping at her pussy to coat my fingers with her cream.

"Oh fuck, Tige, that feels nice," she cried.

While continuing to tongue her clit, I slipped one and then two fingers in her pussy. Her walls clamped down tight on me while I started to pulse inside her, making a 'come here' motion with my fingers toward the front of her tummy.

Wes continued pumping his cock through her

hand, and she ground down against me until I could feel the pulsating of her pussy.

"Oh, oh, god. I'm coming, Tige. Fuck me with your fingers," she said hoarsely, bucking on my hand to the point of nearly breaking it.

But I wanted this woman to experience pleasure —a lot of it—and finger fucked her till her head dropped against her chest and her moans turned into little squeaks.

I lay her on her back on the bed and pointed for Wes to get on the other side of her. Whipping out my aching cock, I started stroking myself, aiming directly at her tits, and knowing I didn't have long before I exploded. But Wes, following my lead, pulled on his own dick a couple more times, and spurted all over Orla's chest before I did.

My balls tightened as a drop of perspiration ran down my temple. But I didn't stop, and lay my cum right on top of the mess Wes had left, all over our lovely lady's breasts.

After cleaning her up, we slipped her between the covers, each of us taking an opposite side.

15

TIGE ST. JAMES

"Somebody had a good night last night," Apollo said, shaking his head.

"You would be right about that," Wes said, passing around the coffee he'd just made.

Which meant we'd be going *out* for coffee shortly. Wes couldn't make coffee to save his life, and with Orla home sleeping, we weren't going to have her magic touch around the office for another hour or two.

Apollo grimaced after he took his first sip, and Wes howled with laughter. "You guys are such pussies when it comes to coffee."

Apollo went to the kitchen and dumped his down the drain. "Anyway, I came home last night to a completely dark house and the sound of you two fuckers snoring in the guest room. Poked my head in and saw three of you having sweet dreams."

I choked down the last of my coffee. "You have no idea how fucking sweet it was." The night I'd had with Orla, when we first met, had been great, but this time it was fucking outstanding.

And I didn't get kicked out the next morning, which would have been hard to do anyway, since it was my home.

I had a boner just thinking about it all again.

I could have spent all day recapping the night, but it was time to get to work. "Guys. Let's talk about Orla's case. Wes, you have some information to share?"

He nodded. "I do. Turns out the stepsister has left town."

"No shit," Apollo said. "How do you know that?"

Wes smiled. "I have my ways."

And whatever his 'ways' were, I wanted to know nothing about them.

"So what are our next steps—"

The front doorbell jingled and all heads turned to watch Orla bound in, grinning brightly.

I was especially glad to see her smiling because

personally, I couldn't wipe the happy expression off my own face.

"Morning," Orla said, blasting through the lobby where we were meeting.

She disappeared into the bathroom and returned in different clothing. "Hey, guys. Look. I had some money left over from the five hundred bucks you gave me. This is what I bought."

She did a little spin, and then stopped, waiting for our comments.

But I wasn't sure what to say.

"Um, Orla, you went shopping and that's what you bought?" Wes said.

She looked down at her form-fitting pants and tank top. 'Yoga clothes,' I think they were called.

"Is there something wrong with them?" she asked, puzzled.

Well, shit. Not if you want the world to see every nook and cranny of your delicious, curvy body, including the three men you work with who were already drooling over you.

I headed to my desk. "You look fine, Orla. Hope you had a good night's sleep."

She blushed at that, which of course made my dick twitch. Again.

Jesus, what this woman did to me.

"Orla, would you mind making some real coffee

for us? Wes attempted it, but nearly poisoned us," Apollo said, laughing.

"Oh, sure," she said, skipping back to the kitchen.

Jesus, she was in a good mood.

And I could think of many more ways to ensure she stayed that happy. It was funny, but I was no longer pissed about missing my vacation.

This shit was turning out to be much more fun.

16

ORLA FELLOWES

"Hello. May I help you?"

After I'd made coffee for the guys, I took my seat at the office's front desk and attempted to organize the mess the previous admin had left. Thank god she'd won a Vegas jackpot because I doubted, from the work she left behind, that she had the skills to do much else.

But hey, it meant I had a job, at least for the short-term.

Our front door buzzed, and I looked up to see an attractive, mature woman clutching her bag. I let her in and noticed she didn't look happy.

"Hello," I said, with my brightest smile. "Welcome to St. James and Associates. I'm Orla."

Her shoulders relaxed a little at my greeting. "Hello," she said, shaking my hand. "I am um, Louise French from the downtown boutique, French Kiss."

No. Way.

"Oh! I know that boutique. Haven't been there in ages, but you have lovely things. So tell me, what is in for this season?"

But from the look on her face, she wasn't here to talk about fashion.

Her chin quivered, and her eyes got glassy.

"Oh, Mrs. French, come sit over here," I said, leading her to the sofa in the lobby.

I took her hand. "Tell me what's going on," I said.

She sighed, and looking up at the ceiling, one big fat tear rolled down her cheek. "Well, you might know, I've had the shop for twenty-plus years," she said.

I nodded. "Yes, I remember going there growing up. French Kiss. It was the store all the girls couldn't wait to shop at when we got older. Such beautiful clothes."

"Thank you."

"So, what brings you in, Mrs. French?"

She shook her head sadly. "Well, for the first time in all my years of business, I have inventory that is going missing." She caught a little sob and another tear rolled down her cheek.

"Oh, no. That's terrible. What's missing, and when did it happen?"

We heard footsteps and looked up to see Tige standing in the lobby doorway. "Excuse me. Orla, can I see you for a sec?"

"Mrs. French, will you excuse me for just a moment?"

She nodded tearfully as I left her to follow Tige to his desk.

"Hey," he said quietly, "you're not licensed to discuss cases with clients. So just be careful what you say in terms of making commitments."

Shit. I hadn't even thought of that. "I'm so sorry. I guess I was just thinking I could relate to what she was talking about, and I got kind of carried away. Poor thing, she's so upset."

He waved away my concerns. "Don't worry, sweetie—"

Shit, he'd just called me sweetie…

"—you are doing fine. Very compassionate. You know, we've never considered the advantage we might gain from having a female on our team. It could open a world of opportunities."

Yeah, opportunities like the one I'd had the night before with Mr. Doe, AKA Don Johnson.

But I didn't want Tige getting any ideas. "Not sure I'm down with something like that. Just trying to help out. Sorry if I overstepped."

He shook his head hard. "On the contrary. I am very happy you took the initiative. You're a natural with people."

Well.

After Mrs. French left, with a commitment from me that I would meet with the 'real detectives' and look into her situation, I broke down and finally called Jenni. I couldn't sleep on the office sofa one more night, and I knew better than to assume I had a permanent place at the guys' house.

I was just going to have to tell her everything. She was my BFF and could deal, even if she were in the throes of planning an event to rival a royal wedding.

But when I dialed, the call didn't go through. Instead, I got a weird recording that said to call my cell phone carrier.

After going through a torturous question and answer tree, and loudly demanding *agent please* more times than I could count, I got a human on the line.

"Hello. I just went to use my phone and the call wouldn't go through."

I heard typing in the background. "Let me check on that for you, Miss Fellowes."

I was put on hold, left to listen to an old Huey Lewis song.

But not for long. "Miss Fellowes, thank you for holding. It looks like you have been removed from Joseph Libby's mobile plan."

I took a deep breath. As much as I felt like it, it wouldn't do to scream my bloody head off. "I… I'm sorry?"

"You are no longer on Mr. Libby's plan. Would you like to set up your own account?"

Holy shit. Joey—the ex—had kicked me off our shared cell service. I was going to kill him. That's all there was to it. "Well, yes I would, considering I enjoy using my cell phone from time to time."

My snark either went over the agent's head, or she chose to ignore it. "All right, Miss Fellowes, we'll need your social to do a credit check, unless you want to opt for a pay as you go plan, which requires a credit card—"

That was it. I'd had it. I couldn't have provided the woman the information she was asking for even if I wanted to, because for the umpteenth time in a week, I was once again in tears.

And I was so fucking tired of it.

So. Tired.

"Orla. Is something up?" Wes asked when I ended the call without even a goodbye.

I hung my head. "Oh. Just found out the ex booted me off our cell plan. So I need to figure out that shit."

I looked back up at him and forced a smile. And in spite of my little pity party, there was a little clenching in my core as I thought back to last night.

His cock had felt so nice in my hand. In fact, I wouldn't mind trying it in my mouth...

Focus.

"No kidding. What an asshole," he said, towering over my desk. "He didn't give you a heads up?"

I gave a half-hearted laugh. "Nope, and now I have no cell phone service."

Wes held a finger up. "Wait right here."

Yeah, like I had anywhere to fucking go.

He came rushing back. "Here you go. We have a whole drawer-full of burner phones. We can also put you on our plan if you like. You know, if that would help?"

Really?

What did I do to deserve these guys? They'd been so endlessly kind to me.

"God, Wes, I don't... know what to say," I said, my voice cracking.

Because of course.

"It's all good. You know, a lot of people have helped me, Orla, when I've been kicked in the teeth. It's nice to do it for someone else for a change."

In spite of his burliness, the kindness in his eyes screamed compassion. That melted my heart a little.

Actually, a lot.

"Thank you, Wes. You're amazing. All you guys are. This help you're giving me—well, it's just for the short-term, okay? I'll get my feet back under me and figure out what the hell my stepsister is up to, that horrible bitch."

Ugh. I hated calling women bitches. But it seemed like the ideal word in a case like this.

He reached to smooth a piece of hair off my face. Such an intimate gesture was something you normally wouldn't do at work. But I guess after the previous night, the usual formalities were out the window.

"I know what it's like to get back on your feet," Wes said. "Earlier in my life I went through a phase of making a lot of bad decisions. But I got past that. I never thought I'd be where I am today. I have a lot of people to thank for that, including Tige and Apollo."

Apollo came around the corner, pulling on his jacket. "You have us to thank for what? Kicking your ass into shape?"

Wes patted him on the back. "Dude, you are

lucky *I* don't kick your ass into shape. Because you seriously need it."

"Fair enough. Hey, everyone, get your coats. We're going to head out to a nice dinner and celebrate."

"Celebrate what?" I asked.

Apollo shrugged. "Do we need a reason?"

17

ORLA FELLOWES

"Hey, I heard you did a good job as bait the other night."

I took a sip of the scotch the guys had served me, now that we were back at their place after our amazing dinner. Damn, it had been nice to be out at a good restaurant.

I set down my glass. "Well, you saw the shape I was in when I got back to the office. But it all turned out okay."

Especially when we'd gotten home later.

I beamed at Apollo. While he—and all the guys, really—had gotten me into that questionable situation, I wanted him to know I was grateful he'd taken matters into hand. Not that I would expect anything less.

"You handled yourself like a champ, baby," he said, raising his glass to me.

I didn't feel too much like a champ.

After the day's earlier cell phone debacle, I'd chickened out again about calling Jenni. I mean, at some point, she was going to wonder where the hell I was. Even in the midst of her wedding planning obsession, she'd eventually call me and freak that my old number—the one I'd had for *years*—was no longer in order.

I was going to have to level up with her at some point about all the crap that had been going down.

I wasn't ready just yet.

But, I was ready for one thing.

I looked around the guy's expansive living room and at the hot detectives surrounding me, starting with Tige, whom I'd obviously, um, met first. The sandy blond hair and combination baby-face-studly-dude looks had gotten me that first night, and by some stroke of luck, I hadn't been able to shake him yet.

Then there was Wes, who had some mysterious, scary background I was yet to hear all about, but who was really a big teddy bear with his shaved head, tats, and piercings. Shit, it had been his idea to comb the tangles out of my hair after my bath that time. No dude had ever offered to do that for me before.

And last was the sensitive, thoughtful Apollo, with his wild black hair and mesmerizing blue eyes, who'd pounded Mr. Doe into the ground when he put his hands on me. I'd overheard the guys talking that he'd possibly jeopardized his case, risking an assault charge, but he explained he didn't care. He never had any doubt about putting me first.

These men were gorgeous and sexy as hell, and most importantly, stepped up to help me when I was pretty freaking down and out. And they hardly even knew me.

Wes winked at me, and the familiar clenching between my legs returned. "Guys, our pretty little Orla should stay with us again tonight. In fact, I think she should stay in the house as long as she wants. We have plenty of room. To hell with the office sofa bed. I wouldn't wish that on my worst enemy."

My eyes darted from one to the next. While it was a generous offer, I wasn't sure it was the best idea. Although last night after my bath and… fun time with Tige and Wes… I'd probably slept better than I had in I didn't know how long.

I didn't have any other options, so why not? At least until I figured out my next move. My dad was due back from his safari any day now. He'd surely override that awful Tawny.

Speaking of which, I needed to ask the guys what was up with all that. I'd done my best to push it out of my mind but I couldn't do that forever.

But at this very moment, I had more interesting things on my mind.

"That's very generous guys. I don't know how I can repay you for all you've done for me."

That's when, just as I'd planned, wicked grins were shared across the room.

Apollo kicked back in his leather club chair, and if I wasn't mistaken, made a quick move to adjust himself in the crotch department. "I can think of a few ways," he said, eyes glinting.

I propped myself on the edge of my chair. I was buzzing, like an electrical current was running through me, and I could hardly hold still. My fingers tapped against the chair's arms, and my high heels clicked on the floor like chattering teeth.

Had the guys noticed?

I couldn't give a shit. They needed to know.

I wanted them. Now.

So, I got to my feet and sauntered over to Apollo, who remained relaxed in his chair, one corner of his mouth turned up in a way that made me feel beautiful and desired.

With his eyes heavily lidded, he looked me up and down like he was just seeing me, assessing me, checking me out, for the first time.

I stared right back at him, my expression serious. I couldn't describe the exchange between us other than saying it was desperately carnal. And incredibly focused.

I reached for the tie belt on my dress, the slinky red one I'd worn the night we'd set up Mr. Doe, and pulled it slowly. I knew it was the only thing holding my wrap dress closed, and that once that small piece of fabric keeping my dress cinched around my body was released, it would fall open and reveal everything I wanted to give the guys that night.

18

WEST 'WES' LANGLEY

WELL, I'D BE DAMNED.

Our little Orla had just dropped her dress to the floor, leaving her standing there in nothing but a sheer little thong panty, a matching bra that barely held her tits, and sky-high heels covered in glittery little rhinestones.

In a word, she was perfection.

And my cock was fucking killing me, trapped as it was in my boxers and trousers.

But this was Apollo's moment. I wasn't going to risk taking anything from him. So I held as perfectly still as possible, even though every fiber of my body

119

was screaming to jump to my feet and devour the almost-nude woman before me.

"C'mere, baby," Apollo growled quietly.

With her back to me, I could appreciate the smooth round globes of her perfect ass that I'd enjoyed the night Tige and I had our fun with her. We'd been so fucking worked up and frenzied I'd never taken a long, slow look at her from head to toe.

Now was my chance.

She leaned over Apollo where he sat in our living room. Placing one hand on each of his shoulders, she folded forward until she was nearly ninety degrees bent. This gloriously left her with her head lower than her ass. The skinny thong string that ran between the cheeks of her ass eased slightly between her pussy lips where it was super-narrow, gifting me with a glimpse of her perfect little asshole.

I'd been around. That was no secret to anyone. I'd had threesomes, foursomes, and more-somes in my younger days. But I'd never seen a woman as fucking hot as Orla.

She was smolderingly sexy, but I think what pushed me over the deep end was that she didn't even have to fucking try. The girls I knew from the street back in the day? They did everything they could to shove their stuff in our faces. In that world, the bigger and burlier the guy you're with, the better protected you were. It was a fact of life. A matter of survival. So the women competed for our attention. It wasn't pretty.

But Orla had no such designs on us, other than to have a good time.

When I'd watched her long enough, ass up in the air while her wild curly hair curtained her and Apollo, I got to my feet and made my way toward them.

I reached for a hank of her hair, coiled across her back, and twirled it between my fingers.

At my touch, she shimmied slightly, shaking her ass against my thigh.

"You good, baby?" I asked before I helped myself to what I was so hungry for.

She turned her head slightly. "I am, Wes," she whispered.

I glanced over my shoulder at Tige, who wore the biggest shit-eating grin I'd ever seen on him, and hooked my thumbs in the strings of Orla's thong, slowly peeling it down below the cheeks of her pretty ass.

With the fabric out of the way, I flicked my tongue over her puckered little hole, which I'd been dying to taste since the second I got a peek of it. She sighed and pushed back against me, a sure sign she wanted more.

She shifted for a moment as Apollo kicked her feet apart. He hoisted her up to straddle his lap with one knee on either side of his hips, and zeroed in on her tits.

From behind her, I returned my tongue to her eager ass, starving for her salty, musty tang. I reached around her slim hips, gently prying her pussy lips apart, finding her soaked with excitement. She was engulfed by my mouth and arms, and I'd never known anything quite so fucking hot.

I continued lapping her ass and playing with her pussy until I fit one and then two fingers inside her. I took that moist cream and brought it back to her asshole, which was beginning to loosen from my attentions.

When I'd gotten it wet enough, I pushed a finger in to the first knuckle, holding it there until her groans subsided. A movement to the left caught my attention, and I realized Tige had moved in for a closer look after cranking the music on the stereo.

Couldn't blame him.

I got to my feet, my legs cramping from squatting for so long. I reached forward and gathered Orla's hair in my hand, pushing it over her left shoulder and watching Apollo play with her tits. Then I leaned next to her right ear.

"Baby, I'm gonna fuck you now. I'm gonna fuck you in the ass, okay?"

She gasped and arched her neck until she could nearly turn to face me. "Yeah, Wes. Fuck me in the ass."

I'd never dropped my pants so goddamn fast.

I didn't like ass sex without lube, but fuck if I was going to stop long enough to run to my room to get some. So, I rubbed Orla's plentiful juices on myself and then her. Satisfied everything was wet enough for our girl to get off, I leaned her forward onto Apollo and pressed the head of my dick against her tight hole.

"Push back baby. Let me in," I said, gripping her hips with my free hand.

Like a good girl, she bore down against my cock, and I slipped inside until my head was buried and she squealed.

But I stopped there. I wasn't going any further until she let me know she wanted me to.

And she didn't waste any time. Her head bucked like a horse, and she pushed back against me, taking another inch in her tight ass. I squeezed my eyes shut against the pleasure that was so intense, it actually hurt. My balls constricted, begging for release, but I held back.

I wanted to hear my girl come.

"You good, darlin'?" I asked, catching Apollo's gaze. He was holding her bent, watching me over her back.

"Yeah," she breathed.

"Can you take more?" I asked.

She nodded. "Yes. Please. More."

She was begging.

So I drove forward while she pushed back and when I was nearly balls deep, began to pulse in and out.

The view of my cock invading her ass was beyond beautiful, and before long she was relaxed enough for me to pummel her like they write about. I felt her contract, almost squeezing me to the point of pain. She pounded her fist on the arm of the chair, screaming as she came.

Her intense reaction, of course, led to my own. My balls tightened, and I exploded into the depths of her ass, pulling out of her tight hole only when I was too sensitive for any more sensation.

The three of us helped her straighten up. We walked her to the bathroom, where I ran a hot bath for her and jumped in the shower myself.

And before I was even done, I was ready to go again.

19

WEST 'WES' LANGLEY

"I HAVEN'T BEEN HERE IN YEARS."

I pulled into the lot for French Kiss, and Orla looked like a kid in a candy shop, checking out the boutique's expensive front windows before we'd even exited the car.

Just as she started to jump out, I grabbed her and pulled her back in. "Hold on a sec, cowgirl. Let's talk about how we're going to do this."

She grimaced. "Of course. Right. Sorry, I got ahead of myself."

Hell if she wasn't adorable. I had half a mind to take her right there in my car…

But duty called, and we'd promised Mrs. French that we'd try to get to the bottom of whatever was going on in her store.

"Ok. This is how we're going to do it," I said, looking Orla right in her eager eyes.

"Yeah?" she asked.

"You'll go in and say you need something for an evening event. Then just start trying some things on, and keep your eyes and ears out for anything of interest. I'll join a few minutes later and say I'm looking for something for my wife."

She nodded. "Got it."

I continued. "Again, we don't know each other. We don't break cover until we absolutely have to."

She put her hand on the door handle again, and again, I took her arm. "Orla. Slow down. They don't open for another few minutes."

She laughed. "Oh my god. What is wrong with me? I guess I'm just excited to really be helping you out. And to help Mrs. French."

I was excited, too. For a number of reasons. I looked at my watch. Five more minutes.

I glanced across the parking lot at the boutique. In the few minutes we'd been talking, the lights had flicked on, and the door had been propped open.

"Time to take the stage," I said, offering Orla a high-five.

But instead, she leaned forward and placed a big kiss on my lips. "I'm on it, boss."

She laughed and hopped out of the car.

Through the crackly sound of the wire we'd placed in her purse, she was greeted as she entered the store.

"What can I help you find, Miss?" a man's voice said.

A man working in a women's boutique? Interesting.

"Oh, hi. I'm looking for something for a formal event I have coming up. I just love this shop. Haven't been here in years."

She was good. So casually conversational.

"Glad to have you back," he said. "Our evening dresses are right over here. Do you have anything in particular in mind?"

I heard clothes hangers squeak across a rack.

"Oh. This red one is nice," Orla said.

Yeah baby. Get the red one.

She looked so goddamn good in red.

Focus, asshole.

"Let me put these in the fitting room for you," the man said.

Good girl. Try on a bunch of stuff so you can stay in there longer.

Just then, I received a text from her.

i'm going to show him the dresses, see what he says

okay, coming in now, I responded.

This might not lead to whomever was stealing from French Kiss, but I was sure I'd be able to help Orla walk out of there with a gorgeous dress or two.

20

ORLA FELLOWES

"That dress sure does suit you."

I turned in the boutique's three-way mirror, checking to make sure the red halter dress the sales-clerk had helped me choose covered all my important bits, and left enough exposed to be alluring at the same time.

It was a winner. And the guys would love it.

Wait a minute. I wasn't here to choose a dress the guys would or would not like.

Idiot.

But the heavy red silk draped nicely over my boobs, and the deep-V accentuated their inner swell.

It was low-cut in the back, nearly to my ass crack, and swirled glamorously around my legs when it moved.

And I had nowhere to wear it. Why was I getting so excited?

Regardless, I felt like a freaking movie star. Mrs. French had clearly not lost her knack for bringing gorgeous clothes into the boutique.

Out of the corner of my eye, Wes entered the shop, his rough burliness out of place in such elegant surroundings.

I pretended not to notice him, but the sales clerk did not.

"May I help you, sir?" he asked, getting closer to Wes than he really needed to.

Good lord. Did this guy really think he could take on Wes if he were the criminal he looked like he might be?

"Yes, you can, thank you," Wes said as I flipped through another rack to listen in. "I'm looking for something for my wife. We have a special event coming up and I… want to surprise her."

The clerk's expression changed when he realized he might make some money off Wes.

"I can definitely help you with that. In fact, my shopper right here is looking for a dress for a special occasion as well."

I cordially nodded at Wes and went back to my search.

"If you'd like to look through this collection over here, sir, I can be with you as soon as I finish up with this lady."

"Great. Take your time," Wes said.

While the clerk had been talking to Wes, I'd taken a look around the shop. It looked like the only way to sneak things out was if someone was in the shop alone.

Like this guy was.

"You know, I think I might go with this dress," I said, gesturing at myself.

The clerk took a step back. "I have to agree. It's absolutely stunning on you. I'll tell you what," he said, moving closer.

"Yes?"

"You can keep the dress if you agree to go to dinner with me," he said smugly.

No way. This guy took a job at a fancy boutique for the purpose of picking up women?

And he gave them free clothes?

This was the person stealing from Mrs. French? Cripes, who would have thought it was a dude?

He inched even closer. So I inched back.

"Oh, that's very generous, but I don't see how I

could accept. I mean, wouldn't that be"—I lowered my voice—"stealing?"

He dropped his head back and laughed. "Oh no. Not at all."

I bet that's not what Mrs. French would say.

So I gave him a demure smile. "Do you do this for all the girls?" I giggled.

He beamed. "Only the beautiful ones," he said in my ear. "But, you can't tell anyone."

I feigned surprise. "But why not? I can't even tell my *beautiful* friends?"

He shook his finger in my face as if I were a bad girl. I wonder how many women in town were wandering around in free clothes from French Kiss.

"If you did, the owner would have me by the nuts."

Well, duh.

"Why do you do it then?" I asked innocently.

"Because beautiful women like you deserve beautiful things."

He picked up my hand and just as he was about to brush his lips across it, Wes jumped out of his chair with his phone to his ear.

"Buddy, you've just given away your last dress. The cops are on the way and you'll be under arrest in minutes."

The clerk looked toward the door, but Wes stood

between him and it. He was apparently smarter than I'd given him credit for, because he realized attempting escape was futile.

"You okay, Orla?" Wes asked.

The clerk's eyes widened. "*You* were in on this? Why you little—"

But I cut him off. "Yup. I was in on it. And I'm going to take this dress. But I will be paying for it, not stealing it."

The cops arrived and while they were handcuffing the man, I had to ask him something.

"Can I ask why you did it? You know, steal?"

He looked at me with hate in his eyes. This freaking detective business must take some getting used to. "Because Mrs. French pays me peanuts. If it weren't for me, we wouldn't sell half the stuff we do. The woman owes me. She owes me!" he cried as he was led out the door by the policemen.

Minutes later, Mrs. French came blowing in. "Thank you. Thank you both. I'm sorry to find the source of the theft was a long-term employee, but at least he's gone now."

"Glad we could help, Mrs. French. And I'm glad I found this dress. It's absolutely amazing, and I can't wait to wear it, even if just around the house."

And I couldn't wait for the guys to take it off me, either.

21

ORLA FELLOWES

"So guys, what's the latest with my stepsister, Tawny?"

I'd had lunch delivered, and as we assembled around the conference table, I dug into my cobb salad.

Apollo nodded. "I was just about to bring that up. We found out she's been in Grand Cayman."

"Is she?" I said.

Of course she was. I could just imagine her skinny ass walking up and down the beach in the smallest bikini possible. That was, when she wasn't chasing down some rich dude with a yacht.

Seemed she'd learned a thing or two from her mother about how to land moneyed gentlemen.

What was odd, though, was taking such a sudden trip, especially when she had no back up for the gallery. Like me.

Tige returned from the fridge with cold sodas for everyone. "She is indeed in the sunny Caribbean and in fact is down there with a man. Do you have any idea why she might be there? Or who she might be there with?"

I'd heard Tawny and her mother talk about the Cayman Islands before. "Yeah! My stepmother has a condo there. Maybe she's visiting?"

Tige shook his head. "No. More like laundering money."

I laughed. "What money? As far as I know, my dad was still subsidizing the gallery. I don't even know if she was able to pay herself."

"Oh, she was able to pay herself with the cash she makes from selling the forged paintings she accused you of being behind."

My jaw nearly hit the table. "*What?*"

"After extensive research, we found that the broker she was working with was previously accused of selling forged paintings. He's at it again, and probably got her into it. She realized it was easy money," Wes said.

My head was spinning. "She had all this going on right under my nose? I mean, who makes the fake paintings?"

Tige shrugged. "Apparently, it's a huge business. There are people all over the place, copying paintings in their garage or warehouse. Tawny was shipping them to unsuspecting out of town buyers, and keeping the real one on the wall until someone bought that one. She's going to be buried in lawsuits from all the artists she ripped off."

"That is, when the authorities catch her. If they catch her," Wes added.

Wait till my father learned all this.

"So, why did she accuse me?"

"She figured her luck had run out and that she was close to being discovered. People had started asking questions. So, she blamed you for everything," Apollo said.

I closed my eyes and rubbed my temples. "Incredible. The whole thing is just incredible."

Wes pulled his phone out of his pocket. "I almost forgot to ask. Do you know this man?" he asked, pulling up a photo.

I took a quick look. "Yeah. That's Tawny's brother, Jake. My stepbrother, I guess I should call him. Didn't really know him well."

Wes's eyes widened. "*What?*"

"Yeah. He's her brother. He came by the gallery every now and then. But we didn't tell my dad or stepmother because he was estranged from them. We weren't supposed to have anything to do with him. Tawny was just trying to be nice. Apparently, they hadn't been in touch in years and had recently reconnected. He seemed pretty nice. Although they looked nothing alike."

The guys looked at me, their faces incredulous.

"Well, that's what she told me," I said. "Why? What did you learn?"

Wes crossed his arms. "First, that's not Tawny's brother, Orla. He's the art broker she was working with. And it looks like he was her lover, as well."

Holy shit. Tawny's story was just getting more and more sordid. The guy I thought was her brother was actually her boyfriend? What a weird sack of shit this family was.

Turned my stomach.

"He probably had the forgeries made and got her to distribute them. At least, that's one of our theories."

And she'd set me up when she thought the heat was on. *Little stepsister Orla can take the fall, no problem.* With the cash she had coming in, no wonder Tawny had been able to acquire so much expensive artwork in such a short amount of time.

"I feel so stupid. I didn't even know this sort of practice existed, and there it was, right under my nose."

Apollo reached for my hand. "Don't beat yourself up. Sounds like she was very discreet, and if you didn't know what to look for, it would be hard to identify."

So. That was all well and good. But how were we going to prove my innocence?

22

APOLLO BECK

"It's been a while. Good to see you."

I bent to give my mother a kiss on the cheek and took a seat opposite her at a coffee shop near the office.

"You too, sweetie," she said, reaching for my hand. "You look well, although you could probably use a haircut."

Our conversations always started this way, with inane small talk and a comment or two about my hair.

I ran my fingers through my mop, which pretty

much no amount of cutting would tame, and agreed with her for the sake of peace.

And ritual.

The only way to end a discussion about my hair was to tell her I had a cut scheduled and that next time she saw me, I would be unrecognizable.

And she'd smile at that, just like she was today.

After we'd broken the ice, that was when we'd get down to the real reason for getting together. And since she'd called the 'meeting,' it was anybody's guess as to what she wanted to talk about.

Although, truth be told, I had a pretty good idea of what was on her mind. Some things just don't change. At least not very much.

"You know, honey, I think your father would love to get a call from you some time."

And there we had it. As predictable as the sunrise. And as old as the earth.

I took a deep breath. "I know you'd like to see us… reconciled… but you know how he is, Mom. It's his way or the highway."

Classic narcissist bullshit.

She nodded so sadly, it kind of broke my heart.

But what was a man to do? My father had all but disowned me because he didn't like my career choice. How fucking insane was that?

I mean, I could see if I'd become a criminal and

broken all sorts of laws. Sure, you could cut someone out of your life for that, I suppose. But just because I didn't opt for what was in his mind a 'high-status' profession, he'd decided I wasn't worthy of his time?

Or any other kind of consideration?

That was some serious crazy-making bullshit. And I'd come to terms with it ages ago.

But, like clockwork, Mom brought it up again, usually once or twice a year. Couldn't blame the woman. Who wanted to see their husband and son estranged?

"Mom, he's taken my decision to become a private detective as a personal affront. I'm not sure there's anything I can do to remedy that."

I'd resigned myself to the status quo. Mom, not so much.

She put a spoon into her tea and absentmindedly stirred, like she was trying to think of a solution to an old, intractable problem. Then she leaned toward me, elbows on the table. "I... think he might try holding your feet to the fire sometime soon. I just wanted to warn you, Apollo. Give you a heads up."

Warn me? For god's sake, what was he going to do? Hold a gun to my head?

I gave a sad, weak laugh. "How will he do that, Mom?"

"He…" she looked around and lowered her voice even though we were the only ones in the coffee shop, "knows the Fellowes girl is staying at your house."

Okay. Was not expecting that.

What the actual fuck?

After I'd composed myself, I was able to speak again. "Mom, what does that have to do with anything? It's no one's business. And how the hell does he know that, anyway?"

I considered telling her Orla's story and how she ended up in a bind, but it really *was* nobody's business.

And last time I checked, I was a fucking adult, for god's sake.

"You know your father. He… knows things. Always has an ear to the ground. And while I'm not sure what he plans to do with that bit of information, I wanted to give you the heads up. You know he hates the Fellowes family from way back, something having to do with Dominic Fellowes. He might be upset about your choice in careers, but he'd really be upset thinking you are having anything to do with someone from that family."

I could see that. Dad was not only self-centered, but a vindictive fuck on top of it. Christ, it wasn't bad enough he was in my face about my career choice but now he thought he had a say in the people I allowed in my life?

What a sad, miserable man.

I looked at my mom, the hurt of bearing family troubles weighing heavily on her once-beautiful eyes. She looked tired. And old for her years.

And I didn't think I could do anything about it.

APOLLO BECK

"Oh hey, Orla. Didn't think there'd be anyone here."

She looked up from her desk, smiling, and all I could think about was how my dad was losing his shit over her being in my life.

I mean, what exactly did he think he 'knew?' That she was a client? Or did he know she'd actually become more than that?

So much more.

But now was not the time to be thinking of things like that.

"You don't seem happy to see me, Apollo," she

said, her eyes twinkling.

I laughed. How was it this woman could make me smile even when I was in a shit mood? "I'm just surprised, darlin'. Didn't think anyone else would be here so early. Speaking of which, why *are* you here so early?"

She shrugged. "Wanted to tackle the filing mess the last admin left."

Jesus. If the woman hadn't won a jackpot and off and quit, we might never have known what a lousy job she'd been doing for us.

Another reason to love Orla.

Shit. I'd said *love*.

"So you *are* happy to see me then? Because you don't look too happy."

I propped my ass on the edge of her desk. "I suppose you're right. I mean, about not looking happy. I *am* happy to see you of course. But I have some family stuff going on."

She leaned back in her chair, her face covered in concern. "Really? I'm sorry to hear that. What's up with the fam?"

I decided to skip that part that involved her—no reason for her to be as pissed as I was—and just give her the short version.

"My family… doesn't like my career choice. They feel I should have become a doctor or lawyer. Something like that. Even after all these years, my dad is still gunning for me to make a change."

Orla slowly nodded in understanding. "Damn. That truly sucks. And what's really messed up is how good you are at your work. Like he can't even see that."

If she only knew how much shit he didn't see... because he chose not to. Like how big of a dick he was every day of his life.

She gave a small laugh. "So I guess I'm not the only one with family problems, huh?"

I had to laugh at that one. No one escaped life's shit, I supposed. We all had our own, unique problems.

I guess the way we distinguished ourselves was how we dealt with them.

And at that moment in time, the only way I could think to deal with the stress of the just-beginning day was to lean down and kiss the lovely Orla.

"DAMN. AT IT ALREADY," Wes said as he and Tige bounded through the office door.

Orla and I straightened up like two little kids caught doing something bad.

And that made us all laugh, which felt damn

good. I needed some levity after my morning with Mom.

"Guys, let's all head to the conference room. We have some things to go over," Tige said.

Minutes later, the gang was assembled, and I had to admit it was nice to have Orla in the room. We didn't know how long she'd be part of our 'team,' but for the time we did have her on board, it was pure pleasure.

In more ways than one.

"Hey, I have a question I'd like to ask," Orla said.

Tige nodded at her. "Miss Fellowes has the floor."

She smiled in appreciation. "So. Do you guys believe I'm innocent with regard to this art fraud thing? I never directly asked you that."

She looked at each of us, one at a time.

Damn. She was really asking that.

"Orla," I started to say, "if we didn't think you were innocent, do you think we'd be helping you like this?"

She shrugged. "I guess I just wanted to make sure. I feel so stupid, trusting Tawny, and then believing some guy was her freaking brother when I'd never heard my dad or her mom mention him, not even once."

"Orla, you didn't see any of this coming because it's nothing you would ever do. You don't lie, cheat, steal… or any of those things your stepsister seems to be so good at," Tige said.

"Speaking of being good at criminal activity, we found that your stepsister, whose real name does not seem to be Tawny, has quite the record."

Orla looked like she might vomit. "W… what kind of record?" she stumbled. "Like she's a crook or something?"

"Pretty much," he continued. "She has a record of petty crimes that crisscross the country. Seems like your stepmother covers for her, tries to get her out of trouble, and then she just does it all over again."

She hung her head. "My father has no idea, I'm sure."

"I bet you are right," Wes said.

Orla dropped her head into her hands. "Good lord. If she hadn't accused me and drawn attention to her scam, who knows when she might have been discovered. My poor father. He tries to help someone out, and this is what he gets. A crook for a stepdaughter, who's running an illegal operation out of a place with his name on the lease."

"She's a professional grifter, sorry to tell you, Orla," Tige said.

She rolled her head around on her shoulders and winced.

"You got a stiff neck, baby?" Wes asked.

She nodded. "I guess it's to be expected."

"Well, let's see what my magic hands can do," he said, crossing the room in a couple large steps, digging his huge fingers into Orla's muscles.

"Oh my god," she murmured. "That feels so amazing. Painful, but amazing."

"Well, I don't want to hurt you," Wes said, brushing her hair aside and running his lips down the exposed side of her neck.

A little smile grew on her face and even though it wasn't even lunch time yet, I could tell there were four people who were already starving.

24

ORLA FELLOWES

"God, Wes, the tension is just melting away."

I rolled my shoulders as he continued digging his thumbs into my shoulder blades and his fingers into my pectoral muscles. Just as his massive hands were capable of doing some damage, they could also heal, apparently.

Some might say he was dangerously close to my boobs, but I was not complaining. And Tige and Apollo seemed pretty happy watching. At least for the moment.

And that moment was short-lived because Apollo came over and lifted me from my chair to lay me back on the conference room table. Without hesitation, he reached under the full skirt I'd bought with the money they'd given me, and pushed my knees up to my chest. Slipping aside the crotch of my panties, he ran his tongue between my pussy lips from clit to ass and back again.

I wanted to come, to forget all the shit raining down around me, and to please these men as much as they wanted to please me. I wanted to let go of all the bad stuff and just feel the good. Close my eyes and float away for a while, even if I were on the conference room table in the office of the detectives trying to prove I was not an art forger.

While Apollo buried himself between my legs, Tige shimmied up on the table next to me and opened his pants. I took his cock in my hand and started stroking, and when I looked to my other side, I found Wes had whipped his out, too.

One gorgeous detective in each hand, and the other between my legs.

I'd never felt sexier.

The four of us moved in a perfect rhythm, Apollo entering me with two fingers, stretching me, opening me, exploring me, and testing me.

He started to pump me harder. "I'm gonna watch you come, baby," he snarled. "And then I'm gonna fuck you till you scream."

Damn. Apollo was a dirty boy.

I turned my head to the side to take Tige in my mouth, smearing his precum over my lips and then going back for more.

A ticklish feeling in my core grew from something tiny, almost imperceptible, to one that spread over me like an incoming wave that couldn't stop. I was prepared to be overcome. Maybe even drown.

And all I could think of was how I wanted more.

As my body convulsed in the first throes of orgasm, I took Tige down my throat with a deep breath until he came in my mouth. I swallowed what I could while my legs thrashed around Apollo, and Wes spurted all over my tits.

The guys moved aside when Apollo reached into his pocket for a condom. Rolling it down his erection, he paused at the opening to my hungry pussy.

"I want to give it to you, baby. Are you good with that?" he said, his voice hoarse, his stare intent.

Some might even say aggressive. I didn't mind. I wanted him in every cell of my body, turning me inside out and upside down.

I nodded. "Yeah, Apollo, I want you."

He gestured at the guys with his chin. "Hold her legs back. Hurry up," he demanded.

"Damn," Wes murmured at the order, but followed Apollo's instructions, anyway.

The guys pushed my knees to my shoulders, and Apollo drove inside me with such force that I shrieked in a combination of surprise and pleasure.

He held himself in place for a minute, no part of me unfilled, before he retreated all the way, leaving me empty and wanting.

He looked down with his gorgeous half-smile, his eyes dark and hooded in a way I'd never seen. Pressing the length of his cock between my swollen pussy lips, he leaned forward and ran his hands up my body. He brushed over my tits and up to my neck, resting on either side of my head. Holding me tightly, he rammed me again, this time not stopping until I screamed, my body jerking in orgasm, and my head unable to move because of the way he was restricting my movement.

He groaned and let go, pulling out of my pussy and ripping off his condom just in time to explode onto my stomach.

He gripped his purple cock, eyes closed, his head dropped back. Veins in his neck protruded like angry cords. Sweat ran off his temples, and wet strands of hair clung to his forehead.

Fucking beautiful.

25

ORLA FELLOWES

THANK GOD THERE WAS A SHOWER IN THE OFFICE because I was covered nearly head to toe in bodily fluids belonging to both the guys and me. I was sticky and crunchy, and ready to be clean.

But I was equally grateful to have a few minutes to myself. I took a seat on the tile floor of the shower and let water stream over my body like a waterfall, and in particular over my sore and battered pussy.

Not that I was complaining.

In fact I was freaking floating.

By the time I emerged from the bathroom, the guys were dressed and chatting on the office sofas, looking like their usual gorgeous selves in their trousers and dress shirts. Tige had on a slim sport jacket like he always did, Wes had his shirtsleeves rolled up above the elbow, showing off his strong forearms and tats, and Apollo was back in his dark wash blue jeans and slim fitting pinstripe vest.

If I weren't careful, I might start drooling, or even worse, tear my clothes back off, and then we'd never get a damn thing done. As it was, it didn't seem like a day when a lot of work was going to be happening.

All three guys looked my way when I clicked into the room in my heels, and they took me in from head to toe, all wearing the kind of approving smiles every girl loves to see from her man.

Or in my case, *men*.

Good lord. I was messing around with three men. Never mind they were working for me, and I for them.

Three of them.

Each wonderful in unique ways that stirred something new in me I didn't even know existed. It was exhilarating, and a little intimidating, all at once.

Regardless, I was going to enjoy it for as long as it lasted, which probably wouldn't be too long. I mean, what guy wants to share a woman with two other dudes?

Although, it was proving to be pretty fucking hot.

Wes got to his feet. "Here she is, our beautiful lady."

In the sweetest gesture, he took my hand.

My heart soared. I couldn't deny it.

Tige came over and planted a kiss on my temple. "Darlin', we were thinking of hitting an early lunch since none of us will probably be capable of concentrating for a few more hours."

Apollo stood before me, staring with an absent-minded smile.

We headed out to Tige's old Mercedes and fifteen minutes later were seated at a great table at the best restaurant in town—on the only day of the week they were open for lunch.

Talk about feeling like a queen.

"Who managed to pull off this small miracle?" I asked, looking over the mouth-watering menu.

"Apollo knew somebody," Tige said, patting him on the back.

"Apollo always knows somebody," Wes added.

He laughed and nodded. "It's true. The Beck family has tentacles that reach into the far corners of this town. Sometimes that's a good thing, and sometimes not."

"Like right now?" a booming voice said from behind me.

I whipped around to see a dashing older gentleman hovering over our little group. As his gaze traveled from one of us to the other, his smile was expansive but his eyes were… cold. As if the bottom half of his face was friendly and the top half was calculating. I didn't think I'd ever seen anything quite like it. An uncomfortable alarm washed over me, like this was a person I didn't want to spend much time with.

Be polite but don't say too much.

He was expensively dressed in an exquisite suit, rocking the silver fox look in a way that revealed he knew he was a handsome older man. Cold eyes and all.

Who the hell was he? And why had he interrupted our little gathering with such an intrusive question?

Wes and Tige looked at Apollo, so I did, too. He seemed a little pale as he stared back, unblinking, at the man.

"Hello, Dad," he said in a tight voice.

No fucking way. This was Apollo's *dad*?

Mr. Beck? The one who detested his son's career choice to the point he'd all but cut him out of his life?

What a creep. I mean, my own family had its

issues, being littered with criminals and all, but at least my dad was on my team.

I swiveled in my seat so I could better see the elder Beck, and after a moment picked out the resemblance between father and son. It wasn't huge, but it was there.

The main difference being the kindness that was always in Apollo's eyes was missing in his father's. It made the younger man infinitely more handsome.

"Apollo. Gentlemen," Mr. Beck said, nodding at each of the guys. "Nice to see you. And this must be the young Fellowes woman," he said, tilting his head and smiling at me.

He knew me? What the hell?

And why was I getting the feeling the whole reason he'd come over was to make some sort of point?

But I wasn't going to let him rattle me, so I extended my hand. "Mr. Beck, nice to meet you," I chirped, pretending the tension in the air didn't exist.

But it did, and it was intense.

He reached to return my shake. "I know your father, Miss Fellowes."

No shit?

"Really. What a small world. He's on safari right now with my stepmother, but he's due to return any day. Apparently they were enjoying themselves so much they added a few more days on Zanzibar—"

Not surprisingly, he interrupted my babbling, looking straight past me to Apollo. "Son, I need you to come by the office this week. I have something to discuss with you."

It was clear he just assumed his wish for a meeting would be granted.

It was also clear he didn't know his son very well. Shit, I'd just met Apollo barely a week ago, and I could better predict his reaction.

Apollo narrowed his eyes. "What do we need to talk about in person? Email has suited us perfectly well for the past several years."

This was one dysfunctional family.

Tige, Wes and I looked back and forth between Apollo and his father like we were at a tennis match waiting for the next volley.

Mr. Beck decided to double down. "If you value your comfortable life here in town, you will find the time in your schedule."

Threatening his own son. What a prince.

Apollo's eyes bore into his father's back as the man returned to whatever hole he had crawled out of.

We all pretended to examine our menus to give Apollo a moment to recover in private. It wouldn't do to pepper him with questions, or even our support, while he was surely processing his dad's unpleasant visit.

Finally, I broke the silence. "Apollo, do you want to take off? We can pick up take-out somewhere and eat back at the office."

He looked at me, clearly grateful for my compassion, and reached across the table for my hands. "No, baby. We are right where we belong. All four of us."

26

TIGE ST. JAMES

I COULD HARDLY WAIT FOR LUNCH TO END BEFORE I could get Orla back to the office and show her what I'd been thinking about for the past two hours.

Of course, I'd been focused on the lunch conversation, much of which had revolved around the unexpected visit we'd been granted by Apollo's father.

It wasn't that we necessarily wanted to spend what was supposed to be a special time together ruminating on what Mr. Beck had up his sleeve and why he suddenly wanted so badly to talk to Apollo in his office. But Apollo and I had grown up together, and I knew enough about his father to know the man didn't do anything unless it served him. It was highly unlikely he'd invited Apollo in order to tell him he was happy that his only son had become a detective, and that he was proud of how he did his work with integrity and honesty every single day.

No, in fact, that was pretty much fucking impossible. Mr. Beck didn't possess those sorts of values.

I didn't want to add to any unpleasantness Apollo might have been experiencing, so I kept my mouth shut about the worst of my thoughts. But I was pretty certain—no actually, I was one hundred percent certain—that his dad was up to no good. And what impacted Apollo adversely, impacted Wes and me.

We guys were tight. It was what made our firm so successful.

So fuck Mr. Beck. That man had been a prick when Apollo and I were growing up, and he'd never changed. Not one bit.

I'd witnessed his disdain for just about everyone on earth, but could brush it off. I'd had a lot of practice. But what I hadn't anticipated, and what had nearly sent me into a rage, was how he'd looked at Orla—like he was some sort of goddamn predator.

The bile rose in my throat when I'd watched him

eye her, like she was a piece of property on display for his pleasure, and when he cut her off to end their conversation so he could try and shake down Apollo, I'd reached the limit of what I could tolerate.

I'm sure I wasn't alone in that feeling.

If he hadn't excused himself and split, I might have had to encourage him to take his leave. And I probably wouldn't have been very polite about it.

While we all tried to pretend otherwise, Mr. Beck's visit had put a damper on our lunch. That's why I was so glad to get back to the familiarity of the office afterwards, when it was just Orla and me. Wes and Apollo took off on a new cheating spouse case.

Yeah, I had our girl to myself.

I went directly to my desk to answer some email, and Orla settled into her own area in the office lobby. She was incredible, always looking for work to do once she'd cleaned up the electronic filing system our old admin had left in a shambles.

I'd forgotten my phone in the car, and when I was about to pass through the office lobby to head outside, I heard Orla on a personal call with the burner phone we'd given her.

I eavesdropped. I'll admit it.

She was talking about us guys. I knew any of the others would have listened in, too.

When I was finally done with my dick move, I

buzzed through the lobby, pretending not to notice anything and by the time I'd returned, phone in hand, I'd decided to ask Orla what was up. She might tell me to take a hike, and if she did, that would be fine. But if she were her usual chatty self, she might open up without hesitation.

She smiled at me as I approached her desk.

"Forgot my phone," I said, holding it up as if I needed an excuse to walk through the lobby.

And see her. Like I did every day.

And when I wasn't with her? I couldn't wait until the next time I saw her.

God, I was turning into a pussy.

"Guess we're all a bit distracted today," she said, raising her eyebrows. "Kind of hard to concentrate after a morning like we had."

She blushed. She actually fucking blushed.

"And then Apollo's dad happening by. How weird was that?" she added.

I didn't know if I would call that *weird*. But I *would* call it unfortunate. Because wherever Mr. Beck went, he seemed to leave a trail of carcasses.

But he wasn't going to touch any of us, not us guys, and especially not Orla. I'd make goddamn sure of that

"I feel for Apollo. He's such a great guy, and just

when he's thinking he distanced himself from his father, the man reappears, making trouble," I said.

The one blessing around Mr. Beck's lurking was that I realized how lucky I was to have the dad I did. Not that we were always best friends, especially during the tumultuous growing up years, but my dad had always let me know the firm would be mine if I someday wanted it, without putting any pressure on me.

In fact he'd called me just the other day. From a fishing boat.

I'd never seen anyone enjoy retirement quite like my father was.

"Tige!" he yelled over the boat's motor. "Interesting news about the Fellowes girl," he said, referring to the recent update I'd sent his way.

"It is an interesting one, Dad. We've never delved into the world of art."

We'd also never met a woman quite like Orla, but Dad didn't need to know the details of that.

"You know, Tige, Orla's dad was one of my first clients when I started the business way back when."

No fucking way.

"What did you do for him?" I asked.

I had a hard time picturing Mr. Fellowes hiring Dad to take care of some sort of cheating spouse case.

Dad yelled for one of the guys who'd just brought in a big fish. "Someone was trying to extort him, saying he was their baby daddy. There were no DNA tests back then, so I had to prove this woman had done the same to at least a couple other wealthy men."

Christ. What a way to get by, claiming fake baby daddies.

"So, the outcome of the case was successful. I remember he was a very nice man. Gracious and humble. I'm sure his daughter is the same."

If he only knew.

"That's pretty wild about your working for the Fellowes family. Orla's father is traveling but when he gets back, I hope he's pleased to see his daughter's with us," I said.

"I'm sure he'll be thrilled, Tige. St. James and Associates didn't earn its strong reputation by sitting around on our asses."

Wow. Since Orla's dad was familiar with the firm, it was going to be *really* interesting when he got back from Africa.

Speaking of which, my thoughts came back to the office, and the reason I'd stopped by Orla's desk.

"Hey, when is your dad due back?"

She gestured toward her computer. "He sent me

an email just this morning. They must finally be in a decent-sized town. Looks like… next Monday."

"Have you told him anything about what is going on?"

She sighed. "I thought about it when I got his email this morning. But I didn't even know where to begin. At the moment," she said carefully, "things seem to be pretty much under control, thanks to you guys, so I want to hold off for a day or so. See what happens. Maybe even wait until he's back."

I wasn't sure I'd take that approach, but if she felt that was best, I could work with that. If I were her, though, I'd at least be dying to get back into my own house.

Not that I wanted her going anywhere.

"So tell me, Tige. You guys are going to prove my innocence, right? I mean, this whole fiasco will just explode apart as the stupidest fucking thing Tawny's ever done. Right?"

Shit. I'd wanted to discuss this with her when I got a bit more information. But she had every right to an update.

"Orla, it looks like Tawny has physical records of your ordering and signing for things."

Her head snapped back. "What? That's not possible."

This was an unfortunate part of the job, letting

people know they'd been set up. "Did you ever sign stuff when you were there?"

She thought for a moment. "Yeah. For sure. I mean, we got regular deliveries of our artists' work…"

Her eyes widened in horror. "No… are you saying… oh holy shit," she moaned, dropping her head into her hands. "I just signed. I never even looked at the paperwork."

I pulled a chair next to hers, and put my hand on her back. "Look, Orla, we are doing all we can here to prove your innocence."

"It's just such a mess," she said quietly.

Now was my chance.

"I heard you talking to a friend earlier," I said.

She looked up at me, her eyes tired. "Yeah. That was Jenni. I haven't told her too much about what is going on because she's completely up to her neck with wedding planning. I didn't want to drag her down with my shit so I kept most of the gallery drama to myself. I sort of mentioned you guys, though."

I couldn't lie. That's what I was most curious about.

"I… wanted to ask you about that. You know, Orla, that night we spent together… that first night?"

"Yeah?"

"I did want to see you again. I didn't intend for it to be just a, you know, hook up."

She wrinkled her face. "Really? Are you kidding?"

I nodded. "It was pretty wild you fell back into my… orbit." I fingered one of her long blonde curls, pulling it straight, then watching it bounce back up.

Time to fish or cut bait. "How are you feeling about things with us guys?" I asked.

"I… I'm not sure. What are *you* thinking?" she asked with a laugh.

"Way to deflect. I'll have to remember that," I said, bringing her hand to my lips.

After I'd kissed her soft skin, I took hold of her hand. "I like you. We all like you. Given the choice, we'd all like to… date you."

There. I'd said it.

She wrinkled her brow, confused. "How… how would that work?"

I took a deep breath. "I'm not exactly sure. But the way it's working right now is pretty fucking hot."

She blushed again, looked at my hand holding hers, and leaned toward me. Our lips met and she melted into me, accepting my tongue as she pulled me closer, her hands on either side of my face.

I pulled back for a moment. I had to look at her.

And damn if she wasn't beautiful. In spite of all the shit she had going on, she still managed to light up every room she entered. Our sweet, kind, brown-eyed girl was also sexy as fuck, taking all three of us guys without hesitation.

She was the kind of girl I could fall for. And that was saying a lot. I had no shortage of women to date, but most of them just didn't do it for me. Guess I was waiting for one in particular. One like Orla.

I had no idea where our current status would take us, and if I said it didn't worry me a little, I'd be a lying motherfucker. I didn't set out to share a woman with my friends and business partners, but in the short time Orla had been on the scene, things were great. Actually better than great.

We guys were working together better than ever, as if something had clicked and our ability to anticipate each other's and the businesses needs were so highly tuned, that sometimes we didn't even need to speak.

It was like a new level of trust had evolved for us.

Had Orla been party to that?

I'd never know for sure. But it was too much of a coincidence for the two things to be unrelated.

With a glance at the front door to ensure it was locked, Orla sank to her knees before me. Glancing up at me with a grin, she unbuckled my belt and unzipped my jeans, reaching through a tangle of boxers and shirt tails to release my aching cock.

And fuck if her hand didn't feel goddamn great.

She stroked me from root to tip, then bent her head to lap up the little drop of precum hanging off my dick. I leaned my head back and took several deep breaths, wanting to make this last a bit instead of exploding like a teenaged minute-man.

But when Orla gobbled me all the way to the back of her throat, I knew it wasn't going to be long —that was the effect she had on me.

I wove my fingers into her curls, not so much to direct her on my cock, but more to just feel her enthusiasm as she dove down on me again and again.

I squeezed my eyes shut and a rumble rose from my chest. Orla grasped my balls in one hand, and deep-throated me so hard I thought I might have a coronary.

I exploded, and she took everything I gave her like a champ. When she came up for air, her eyes were watering and cum was running down her chin.

I'd never seen anything hotter.

27

ORLA FELLOWES

AFTER A DAY OF NOT GETTING MUCH WORK DONE, BUT lots of sexy time, I decided to spend the evening alone, in my room, eating Chinese food and watching an old *Sex and the City* episode.

The guys were fine with that, and they retreated to their own rooms, too, for time to themselves.

And even though I was holed up in my room, propped up on four or five pillows, I loved knowing Tige, Wes, and Apollo were close by—really just a few feet away. It was so comforting and for the first time in a long time, I felt safe and protected. Cared for, too.

I hadn't even known those things were missing in my life, nor that I was craving them. It's like what I needed all along might be falling into my lap after the succession of crappy choices I'd made.

Second chances. We don't always get them, no matter how much we deserve them.

Then, how did I get so lucky?

No freaking idea. I wasn't any more deserving than anybody else. But I was pretty fucking happy about it.

Sure, there were plenty of areas of my life that were a shitshow, like I couldn't get into my own home and had an arraignment hanging over my head. But I believed things would turn around.

Eventually.

Even if Tawny did have my signature on documents that suggested the art forgery she'd pinned on me.

Dad was not going to be happy. He'd been let down by several of his stepchildren, always trying to help like the well-intended guy he was. Later, usually when it was too late, it would dawn on him that he'd been taken, usually for a decent-sized amount of money. Although, it wasn't the money he really cared about. It was the fact that he was always trying to build a family, and some of the people he took under his wings couldn't give a shit that their mother had finally brought a decent man into their lives. They just wanted to see what they could get out of him until mom was on to the next guy.

And now he was married to a woman with a criminal daughter who, if what the guys said was correct, had covered for her wayward child time and again.

I didn't know if that made *her* a criminal, too, but it sure did make her immoral.

And my dad would know all this soon. Very soon.

The next morning there was a soft knock on my bedroom door.

"C'mon in," I croaked, yawning and stretching to get the blood flowing.

"Hey, Orla," Wes said, plopping onto the bed next to me in his plaid PJ bottoms and shirtless top half.

The man dwarfed me, and I don't mean with his endlessly broad chest and huge pecs. He exuded power and dominance with his confident, badass sexiness. Who knew a shaved head, multiple tattoos, and a deep, booming voice would be so damn alluring? A week ago, if I'd seen this man in a dark alley, I'd have turned and gone the other way. Now, it was all I could do to keep from jumping on top of him and grabbing his fat cock.

I mean, he'd been in my room for all of sixty

seconds, and my core was already clenching as I thought back to the time he'd taken me in the ass.

He'd been so gentle at first, and when I'd finally adjusted to his girth, he'd pounded me until I'd come over and over again.

I didn't even know it was possible to orgasm that way.

But shit, if I didn't get those thoughts out of my mind, I'd never be getting out of bed.

So I forced myself to focus. "Make yourself at home, why don't you?" I teased as he stuffed a couple pillows under his head.

He crossed his arms and laughed, all comfy and cozy. "Already did. But thanks for the invite."

I flipped onto my side to see him better. "How'd you sleep?" I asked.

"Great. No, better than great. Although I don't know a word that's better than great so I hope you get my gist."

I nodded. "I hear that. I slept well myself."

"Hey, Orla, I gotta tell you something."

He'd turned serious.

"Tawny's back in town."

I bolted upright in bed. "Really? That's a good thing, right? Or is it a bad thing? Which is it?"

He ran his fingers over my cheek and down to

my jawline. I was pretty sure he was in the early stages of an erection.

Dammit. I hadn't planned on that happening. But on the other hand, what the hell did I think would happen by letting a guy like this crawl into my bed?

"On one hand, it's good because we can track her better, but on the other, it means she's back because she thinks she's untouchable and that her plan to pin everything on you is working."

Fear crashed into my stomach so hard that I clutched it.

Had I really thought things were moving in the right direction?

Why would I think some sort of miraculous progress had been made? It had only been a week since Tawny had me arrested, and while I had no idea how long things involving the law actually took, one week seemed barely enough time for any sort of bureaucratic miracle to occur.

"Is Jake with her?" I asked.

"Not sure about that. And apparently she's not only back but also holding a party in the gallery tomorrow night. And just so that you know, we're all going."

"What? We are? How do you know she's having a party?" I asked.

"I signed up for the gallery email list under a fake account so I can get whatever she's sending out to her clients. She probably wants to sell some more forgeries so she can raise a bunch of cash, and bring it all down to the Caymans on her next trip there."

Well, fuck me. What great news to start the day with.

Just as I was about to thank Wes for spreading the love, he continued. "So, the next bit of news is that we have a really good B&E guy who we're going to have check out some storage facilities we think Tawny's been using. You know, to find the forged paintings"

"B&E?" I asked.

"Oh. Right. This shit is all new to you. B&E is breaking and entering—"

I bolted upright in bed. "Um, we're proving I didn't commit a crime by committing another crime? Is that necessary?"

He held his hands up. "We have to find out where Tawny's storing things. The guy we have looking… well, he's very good. He won't get caught. I know him from… back in the day. The firm calls on him when we need things like this taken care of. We think she might be hiding things in your father's properties, again, to take the heat off herself."

A rage bubbled up in my throat, angering me to the point where it became hard to breathe. I wanted to kill her, plain and simple. Just kill her. It was one thing to try and fuck me up, but to do that to my father?

I shook my head. "I hate her. I just hate her. And when I get my hands on her—"

"Hold on there, Mike Tyson. Before you beat her to a pulp, we need you to behave at least just for one night?"

Oh right. Her stupid gallery party.

"How do you know she won't just kick me out the moment she sees me?"

Wes looked at the clock on my bedside and jumped out of bed, leaving a flash of sadness to sweep over me.

How freaking weird. It wasn't like he was my boyfriend, or anything.

He reached for my hand. "You need to get out of bed and start your day, darlin'. And Tawny probably will kick you out, but hopefully not before we gather some info. We're betting on her wanting to avoid a scene, so this should buy you some time mingling without her interference."

Cool. I could do that. And I hoped she did try to kick me out. I wanted her to create a fuss so I could scream right back at her. Let everyone she knows what a psycho she was.

But even if that didn't happen tonight, it would happen soon enough.

I could feel it.

28

ORLA FELLOWES

Knowing how Tawny liked fancy gatherings, I slipped into my trusty red wrap dress, pushing the girls together for good measure. Then, I strapped on my glittery high heels, swiped on some lip gloss, and drove myself to the gallery.

Where I used to work. And which my dad basically owned.

The guys were already there, pretending to be clients. I'd briefed them on some art patron vocabulary so they could seem legitimate. At least not before they did all the snooping they wanted to.

As I drove across town, I thought how strange it

was for her to just up and leave town, and then return just as mysteriously. When I'd been working at the gallery, she'd left me in charge one time but said she was just going away for the weekend with some friends. I didn't ask anything at the time because I didn't really care who she hung out with. I was focused on making some gallery sales to impress her.

Imagine. There'd been a time when I'd wanted to impress her. Now, I wanted to give her a black eye.

And then, the guys were going to have some cat burglar snoop around for proof Tawny was in the forgery business. It was good thinking—she must be keeping the paintings somewhere.

But I didn't want to know anything else about how they planned to accomplish that. The less I knew about any nefarious tactics, the better.

I parked a few spaces down from the gallery when I arrived. I actually should have parked even farther away, but I knew I couldn't walk far in my heels. I clicked up the sidewalk, my heart pounding, wondering what the evening would bring. Pulling my trench tighter, I walked inside the gallery for the first time since I'd picked up my belongings there.

The evening was in full swing. If there was one thing I could give Tawny credit for, it was that she knew how to throw a nice shindig. The lights were low, the crowd relying on glittering candlelight to navigate the night, and the stereo pusled out some nice, jazzy tunes.

She did not do things half-assed and was a champ at painting herself as one of the town's elite—a status she never would have acquired if not for my father.

And one she was soon to lose.

I draped my coat over a chair by the door in case I needed to make a quick getaway, and immediately saw Tawny in a corner of the room, holding court with several attractive and most likely rich men.

Before she saw me, I slipped into another room and got a close-up look at a couple paintings. I had no way of knowing what was a fake and what was not, and when I examined them up close, they looked perfect to me.

But of course they looked perfect to me. If they were passing muster with real collectors, they'd have to be pretty fucking good copies.

Or maybe they were the real thing? Who knew?

"May I help you?" a female voice shrilled behind me.

I knew who it was. Didn't even need to turn around.

Damn. I'd hoped for more time to snoop. But of course the hawk-eyed Tawny, in her effort to smell out money, had her gaze glued to the front door to get a look at everyone who walked in.

And that included me.

I turned to face her. She looked good. Tanned. Relaxed.

Criminal.

"Tawn," I said, using the nickname she hated, "So glad you're back from… where were you? The Caymans?"

"What are you doing here?" she spat, narrowing her eyes.

Guess I was putting a damper on her party.

I shrugged. "Just… looking. I might want to buy something. But, you know, first I want to make sure it's real. I'm not into the forged paintings you've been so successful at selling. Can you tell me how to tell the difference? I mean, your forged ones are so good."

I moved on to the next painting with her right on my heels and leaned closer to examine it.

"You were not invited. Get the hell out," she said, gritting her teeth.

I glanced over my shoulder. "I know I wasn't invited," I taunted. "So rude of you to leave me out. I mean, my father sets you up with this nice little business, and this is how you treat *me*?"

She took a step closer. "Get out," she said, just a few inches from my face.

But I didn't back down. My anger had pushed me past any kind of intimidation that might rear its lame-ass head. So I further provoked her by shaking my finger in her face. "Tawn, if you're not careful, your patrons will see you're really just a white trash grifter who's trying to rip them off. In fact, I may just make an announcement to everyone here tonight—"

Her eyes narrowed. "Don't you dare."

I dropped my head back and laughed. "Hey, looks like you have a buyer over there," I said, pointing.

Her eyes lit up. "Fine. I'll be back. Just wait here."

"Whatever, Tawn. Now go. Sell one of your paintings. If that's what you can even call them."

29

WEST 'WES' LANGLEY

"I CAN'T BELIEVE PEOPLE CALL THIS ART. I MEAN WHAT the fuck?"

I looked around the gallery, then back to Apollo. "People pay real money for this stuff?" I asked, lowering my voice.

Apollo shrugged. "No accounting for taste, man. Besides, I don't think they're so bad. I like that one over there."

"That one? It looks like some graffiti I painted when I was a kid—"

"Hey," Tige said, returning from the bar with a

club soda, "are you guys flapping your gums or are you keeping an eye on Orla?"

I rolled my eyes. I was in a shit mood. This gallery place gave me the creeps. Bad juju and all that.

In my past life, when something felt off, I'd hit the road. Not so much anymore, though. When something bad was in the air, I had to ride it out. It was what I got paid for.

Didn't help my mood any, though.

What had been nice was watching our girl Orla work her way through the party. She was born for this sort of thing—beautiful and graceful, capable of weaving through the crowded rooms without bumping into anyone or attracting any unwanted attention.

Shit, I wish I could do that. I'd been turning heads all my life, and not in a good way. When a guy looked like me, he elicited a strong response from people. They were curious and wanted to know more—or they hit the road and ran.

But Orla's clingy red dress and crazy blonde curls lifted my spirits as I moved around the party, pretending to like art that looked like a six-year-old had painted it.

Guess this shit just wasn't for me.

I wandered away from the guys, probably feeling

a little too overprotective of Orla, when I realized I'd lost sight of her.

Moments earlier, she'd climbed the gallery stairs to the mezzanine to look down over the crowd. When I'd caught her eye and winked, she'd nodded discreetly.

Her stepsister, recently done glad-handing some poor sucker who was probably going to throw down a pile of cash to take home an ugly piece of shit, ran up the steps after her. I watched them go back and forth. Orla kept her cool while Tawny was losing hers.

But now I didn't see either of them.

What the fuck.

A flood of concern—and a drive to defend—washed over me as the bad feelings I had about the gallery snowballed on me.

I surprised myself, to be honest.

While Orla was an outstanding woman by any measure, I'd sure as hell not known her long enough to go into a rage when she was out of sight.

And yet I was.

Without a word to the guys, I bounded up the steps to the mezzanine level where I'd last seen Orla and Tawny speaking by the railing.

And where we could also keep an eye on Orla.

There was no question we'd stressed that—stay in our line of sight.

But she hadn't.

Once at the top of the stairs, I craned my neck to see over the thick crowd. If I had to hand anything to Tawny, she sure as hell knew how to pack a party. It was a well-heeled crowd, expensive and artsy looking, all sucking down free cocktails and gushing over the art.

Made no damn sense. To me, anyway.

I elbowed through the people, careful to not attract any attention by looking like I was trying to keep a woman safe from her criminal stepsister in the midst of a fancy gallery full of partiers.

But when I'd traveled from one end of the room to the other having avoided stepping on any toes and still not caught sight of Orla or Tawny, my anxiety kicked up a notch.

Goddammit, I'd told her to stay in sight.

Fuck me. I wanted to convince myself she was fine, and that the beautiful young woman I'd watched sleep for a few minutes before I woke her that morning had just run to the ladies' room. But knew better than to make assumptions, especially because of the people we knew we were dealing with.

After all, it was highly unlikely Tawny was the

only person in attendance that night from her 'team' of crooks swindling people by selling them fake shit.

There were other criminals in the crowd. I was sure of it.

And yeah, I had a thing for Orla. I wasn't going to deny it. The guys knew, and if she didn't know by now, she soon would. Not that it mattered any.

Girls like her didn't go for roughnecks like me. It just didn't happen.

But that didn't mean I wouldn't try. And that didn't mean I wouldn't do all I could to protect her, regardless.

I hated to lose a minute searching for her, but I knew we'd all be more successful if I had Tige and Apollo on board. So, I ran back down the stairs, this time not giving a shit about how much attention I might attract.

"She's missing."

The expressions on their faces immediately changed.

"Where'd you last see her?" Tige asked, frowning.

I pointed. "Right up there. By the mezzanine railing."

"Okay. Wes, go back up there to see if she's in the rest room or if maybe there is another stairway leading somewhere. I'll head outside to see what I can find. And Apollo, you scout out this floor and the offices."

We went our separate ways, with me running back up the stairs. I pushed open both the men's and ladies' room doors, hollering for Orla while I checked each stall.

I got some funny looks in the ladies' room, but I didn't give a shit.

After coming up empty, I scraped the perimeter of the room, checking the couple doors I found.

All locked.

Except one I spotted in a far corner, which, from the light shining through it, was slightly ajar.

I ran toward it and once outside, found myself on the building's roof, which connected with the rooftops of the buildings adjacent to it.

"Orla!" I hollered.

Straining to hear over the noise seeping from the party, a faint cry pricked my ear.

"Hey," a woman's voice strained, "over here."

I climbed to the roof of the building next door. "Orla? Where are you?"

I whipped around a corner to find her on the ground, struggling to get up, both her knees and the palms of her hands dirty and bleeding.

"What the hell," I said when I'd reached her.

"Oh my god, Wes, I wasn't sure anyone would

ever find me up here. Thank you," she said, throwing her arms around my neck.

After her embrace, I pulled back to check her out at a glance. "Here. Let me help you up."

But as soon as she got to one foot and tried to put weight on the other, she tumbled toward the ground with only me to hold her up.

"Shit. Twisted my ankle on top of everything else."

My phone rang and I saw it was Tige. "We're up on the roof," I said, then hung up.

I wanted Orla to have my undivided attention. My heart had been pounding like a motherfucker since I'd found her, and even though she wasn't gravely injured in any way, I'd still not calmed down.

I was just about to get her to tell me what had happened when Tige and Apollo came running out onto the roof. "Wes!" they hollered.

"Over here."

They rounded the same corner I had, and joined me on their knees when they saw Orla.

"I was just asking her what happened."

Apollo looked carefully at her raw palms. "Tell us how you ended up here, baby."

She took a deep breath as she tried to straighten out her bloody legs. "I was talking—actually, arguing —with Tawny, when she left me, running across the room to some man. I watched him grab her by the arm really hard. She tried to pull away and the weird thing was, no one else in the room even noticed what was going on. He dragged her toward the door, and I followed."

"You did *what?*" Apollo asked, shaking his head.

"Yeah. Guess I shouldn't have done that. Anyway, I followed them out onto the roof very quietly. I don't think they knew anything, but my heel caught on something and I went down, so I crawled over here to hide. That's how I got all scraped up and I guess twisted my ankle. I'm not sure where Tawny and the man went."

Tige pulled off Orla's shoe and touched her ankle in a couple places, causing her to wince. "I don't think this will be too bad. We'll help you get out of here."

I hoisted one of Orla's arms around my neck and we got her standing on her one good foot.

"You know, you shouldn't have chased after any of those people. You don't know how dangerous they are. If the guy was strong-arming Tawny like you said, it's my guess she owed him money. He's probably armed. You don't want to take chances with that shit," I said.

Her eyes widened as she hobbled between Apollo and me. "Are you kidding? That never even occurred to me. These people are hard core. I'll be glad when we're out of here. I never want to come back."

"Yeah. Let's get the hell out of here," Tige said. "You were brave tonight, Orla. More than you needed to be. Promise us you won't try anything like that again."

She gave a small laugh. "Don't worry about me. I have no hero complex. I'm minding my own business from now on. You guys can do the heavy lifting."

I didn't have the heart to tell her we were only just getting started.

ORLA FELLOWES

"It doesn't really hurt that badly."

I looked down at my slightly purple, slightly swollen ankle and shook my head.

It could have been so much worse.

When we'd gotten home last night, the guys brought me to my room, propped my foot up, and packed it with ice. They knew their first aid.

"Hey, which of you were Boy Scouts?" I teased.

Both Wes and Apollo looked at Tige, who crossed his muscular arms, made even sexier by the sleeves he'd pushed up past the elbow.

Who knew forearms could be so… distracting?

I looked up to catch him giving his friends a serious stink eye. "Yeah, I was a Boy Scout. My dad was one of the leaders."

Oh. My. God.

I could totally see it. Blond, preppy Tige and his scoutmaster dad pouring over first aid books together so he could earn a badge or pin or whatever they gave out.

I'd been a Girl Scout. For about one day.

It wasn't for me.

Apollo burst out laughing, and Wes followed with his own bellowing. "He tried to get me to join, but I was like no way. Even when we were kids I could see that Boy Scouts was for dorks," Apollo said.

I bit my lip. I didn't want to laugh at Tige, too.

Plus, I thought the whole thing was just so freaking… cute.

Here was the guy I'd brought home for a one-nighter, thinking he was just another horn dog I could get my single girl thing on with, and he turns out to be my protector, my employer, and my Boy Scout.

You just never knew what life was going to throw your way.

As I sat looking at Tige, laughing with his friends, my heart cracked open a little as I could see him as a kid, tagging along to work with his dad, eager to learn the business. It was so endearing.

And *normal.*

"What can I say? I like to be prepared," Tige said, taking the ribbing in his stride. "And as you can see, it's paid off. I'll have Orla's ankle back to new in no time at all. More than I can say for either of you two losers."

I looked at Tige to see if he was serious, and when he began shaking with laughter, we all did.

Next morning, I was able to hobble to my car with no trouble at all, and pick up some decent coffee for the guys on the way to the office. I had to admit I got a kick out of getting there before they did, picking up coffee, turning on the lights, and tidying up the place.

It was small stuff, but I was happy I could do something for them.

They'd certainly done a lot for me.

Just then, Tige burst in like his ass was on fire.

"Meeting in the conference room soon as the guys arrive," he said, blowing past me.

Well. Shit.

Apollo and Wes were behind him by only five

minutes, so when they got there, I ushered them into the conference room.

I handed out the coffees I'd gotten as Tige took his usual seat at the head of the table—where he'd sat the first time I'd been there.

"Okay, Wes got some news this morning," he said. "You want to take it from here?"

All eyes were on him. "Heard back from my B&E guy. You know, the one checking out storage facilities we believed Tawny may have used?"

He looked directly at me.

Of course I remembered. How could I forget? In order to prove my innocence, he'd had somebody break the law. I wasn't really down with that, but I also really, really didn't want to go to jail.

"What did he find?" I asked hopefully.

I imagined a storeroom of canvases propped against each other, all copies of the originals we had hanging in the gallery. Tawny would pawn these off on unsuspecting clients who'd be out tens of thousands of dollars. And if all went according to plan, they'd never know.

Wes looked at Tige and Apollo, then back at me.

"Nothing."

I looked around, wondering if I was the only one who had no idea what the hell Wes was talking about.

"Um, what? What do you mean?" I asked.

"My guy checked out the facilities Tawny had been known to use—we got the addresses from going through the gallery's mail—and they were all empty."

How could that be?

"D... doesn't she need to store the stuff somewhere?"

He nodded. "She certainly does."

Apollo leaned his elbows on the table. "We'll eventually find it. You can only hide large paintings in so many places. But what this means in the short term is that it makes it harder to prove your innocence without evidence that Tawny herself is guilty."

What the fucking fuck?

The morning coffee suddenly wasn't sitting too well in my stomach.

How in god's name could it be difficult to prove my innocence? I hadn't done anything except sign some documents Tawny tricked me into signing.

"S... so, what does that mean?" I asked, my voice cracking.

Tige reached out and placed a hand on my arm. "It means your arraignment is coming like a freight train, and that we need to come up with something else."

Something else? What the hell did that mean?"

"I… I don't understand."

"We need you to wear a wire. Get Tawny to incriminate herself."

I could do that. Hell yes. And I wanted to do it sooner rather than later. I wanted to stay out of jail.

"Can we start today?"

ORLA FELLOWES

"Hey Tawny, it's Orla. Can I talk to you for a minute? Please?"

I'd called her from one of our burner phones so she wouldn't know who the incoming call was coming from. And it had worked. She picked up on the first ring, probably believing I was one of her highly-private clients.

"Orla, I can't talk to you. Don't call me again—"

"Wait! Please, Tawny. Just hear me out," I begged.

It was fake-begging, but still.

"What Orla? What the hell do you want?" she snapped.

I could see her, hair scraped back into a bun so tight it pulled on her scheming, beady eyes.

I crossed my fingers. This needed to work, or my problems would be going from bad to worse. "I... I need a few things from the house. I'm desperate, I really am. C'mon. I know why you locked me out but I need some of my things. Especially my... migraine medication."

Okay that was another freaking lie. I'd never had a migraine in my life. But I figured, how could she deny me medication? On the other hand, she was so cold-hearted. She probably wouldn't give a shit if my head exploded right in front of her. She'd probably wipe the mess off her dress and be on with her day.

Big sigh. "Okay. All right. You can come over tonight. But only for ten minutes. And I'll be watching you the whole time."

Yes. Exactly what I'd hoped.

I looked at Tige, who winked at me from across the conference room table.

"Great. I promise to be in and out."

Hours later, I pulled into the circular drive in front of my father's house. It was crazy to arrive knowing I couldn't just open the door and walk in, but if everything went according to plan, that would be remedied sooner rather than later.

I rang the bell.

"I thought you were coming an hour ago," Tawny hissed, holding the door open for me.

"Nice of you to let me in," I chirped, ignoring her side-eye.

I entered the foyer with her close on my heels, discreetly looking around to see if much had changed in the week-plus I'd been banished. On the surface, things were the same, but with Tawny in the picture, anything was possible.

For example, had she discovered the safe in my father's study?

I headed straight up the stairs to my room, but when I passed Tawny's, I stopped dead in my tracks.

"Um, where are you going?" I asked, poking my head into her room.

Her room in my father's house where she, by the way, lived for freaking free.

"Don't worry about it," she said, pulling the door shut.

But not before I saw her entire closet had been emptied into suitcases and the drawers of her dresser were in the process of being packed, as well.

Somebody was leaving town, and it wasn't for a quick jaunt to the Caribbean.

I turned to face her. "Well. Seems like I'm not the only one leaving Dad's house."

She nudged me forward. "Mind your own business. You have ten minutes before I call the cops on you for trespassing."

She had some fucking nerve. Call the cops on me in *my own father's house?*

But I could fight with her about that another day. I was there for one thing, and one thing only.

And it wasn't to grab my things.

Yeah, I'd told a little lie.

When we got to my room, I pulled a duffel out from under the bed and started picking through my closet. Slowly.

"But, Tawny, what about the gallery?" I asked over my shoulder, as if I were really concerned. "You've built such a good business."

Fucking stealing from people.

She huffed, glancing at her watch. "Let my mom and your dad figure that out. I'm done with the gallery. Now get your shit and hit the road."

"Why the rush? You expecting someone?" I taunted, holding a pretty piece of jewelry in one hand and a cashmere sweater in the other.

Bait. Something I knew a little about.

She stood in my bedroom doorway, tapping her foot. "I told you. Mind your fucking business."

I smiled sweetly at her. "You're right. I just can't help it. I'm a big old nosy body. Hey," I said, dangling the expensive necklace in front of her.

"I don't want this anymore. It's gold. You want it?"

Her eyes widened.

"Yeah." She snapped it up without hesitation, rolling it over in her fingers, probably assessing its worth.

Next, I held out the sweater. More bait. "I don't want this either," I said, turning up my nose. "It's cashmere. You want it?"

"Yeah." She grabbed it, also.

I held up a pair of Louboutin heels.

She was practically drooling.

"Do you want to tell the police that you forged art and tried to set me up for it?" I said, in exactly the same tone.

And just as she reached for the shoes, she stopped, looked at me, and frowned.

That's right, bitch.

"What?" she said, confused. "Why would you say that?"

I just stood there looking at her, smiling sweetly, still holding the shoes.

She pointed a finger at me. "You need to get over yourself and grow up. Learn the ways of the world."

"Oh. So you did do it then," I said, taking small steps toward her. "How could you? My father set you up in that business. You cheated people, and look how you treated your own stepsister."

I continued inching toward her. I couldn't stop. The guys had told me to stay away from any physical altercation with her, but it was like my legs had a mind of their own.

The rage I'd kept bottled up for the past week was bubbling over like a boiling pot. It had a mind of its own just like my legs. And it wasn't going to be contained.

I realized I finally had the upper hand when Tawny's eyes widened and she took a step back. "You have no idea what you're talking about."

"C'mon, Tawn. I also know the guy you claimed was your brother, was someone you were sleeping with *and* the person feeding you the forgeries."

Her phone buzzed and when she looked at her text message, her face paled. "I… I really need to go now. That means you do too," she said, grabbing my arm.

So I sat on the edge of my bed, dragging her with me. "Hey now," I said. "I'm not done going through my things. Like these Louboutins here. I'm just not sure I should keep them…"

Whatever had been in that text message had changed her demeanor entirely.

"Orla, please. We have to go. You can't stay here."

I wrinkled my brow. "Why, Tawn? What did you do?" I asked.

Her eyes were darting and she was starting to shake. "Look. I had no choice…"

And there we had it. I touched the wire the guys had attached to my bra, as if to make sure it was still there. I had no way to confirm they were hearing everything okay. I just had to trust things were working the way we'd planned.

I steadied my wobbly breath. "Okay. You've admitted it. Now wait until everyone else finds out about what you did, too. You should be ashamed of yourself."

Now that she'd made her confession, wouldn't the guys come running in? I mean, they'd heard her too, right? That was the next step.

But where were they?

Oh no. What if the wire hadn't worked? Had I just gotten Tawny to admit to her shit for no reason at all?

While I was starting to panic, the expression on Tawny's face turned dark and ugly.

"I had no choice, Orla, and I have no choice right now."

APOLLO BECK

"Where the hell did she go?"

We were down the street from Orla's father's house, listening over the wire we'd set her up with, and were psyched when she'd gotten Tawny to start admitting to what she'd done.

I knew Orla could do it. She was a natural.

But when we heard a *thud*, like a body falling to the floor, and Orla stopped speaking, the warm happy feeling that came with success withered. A chill whispered over me and my pulse began to race.

Could be good news or bad. For a fleeting

moment I hoped she'd taken out Tawny. The woman deserved at least that much.

But in my heart, I knew better. Orla probably wasn't capable of slugging someone, no matter how pissed she was. But I'd bet money that Tawny *was*.

And now it seemed like the worst had happened.

Shit, shit, shit.

Tawny had done something to Orla. I knew it. The woman was desperate—probably why she was leaving town—and wasn't about to let her stepsister, who wasn't much more than an annoying detail, get in the way.

If something had happened to Orla, well I didn't know what I'd do. I had it bad for the woman. I couldn't deny it.

Without exchanging a word, Wes, Tige and I were out of the car, running toward the house within seconds of Orla going silent. Once on the property, we rounded the north side of the house as Orla had briefed us, found the kitchen door, broke the window on it, and headed for the stairs.

Alarm coursed through me, leaving my temples pounding in a way that was not at all pleasant. But it revealed something important.

This was a different sort of case for me. Not so much the gallery or the art world, although those were definitely a first. What really diverged from my previous work was how *involved* I was in this case. *Too* involved, some might say.

Tige and his dad always said to stay objective about your work, no matter how much something pulled at your heartstrings. Or how beautiful a client might be. And until Orla, I thought I'd done a good job of that. Keeping my heart out of the work by seeing myself as a conduit to the truth. The work I did enabled people to make important decisions about their lives.

All that had flown out the window pretty much the moment Orla came to our office.

I'd admit it. I was a little envious Tige had a night with her first. If that had been me, I wouldn't have left without her phone number.

Orla was not the kind of woman you let slip through your fingers.

But I had her number now. We all did.

How lucky was I?

How lucky were we all?

And did she feel the same?

Taking two steps at a time, I was in the lead, and when I reached the landing, caught a glimpse of Tawny sneaking around the corner at the end of the hall. When she realized I'd seen her, she took off running.

"Where's Orla?" Wes shouted, sticking his head in one bedroom after another.

In the meantime, Tige took off after Tawny.

"She's here. Orla's here!" Wes called.

Tige hesitated, but I waved him on. "I'll check on her. Get Tawny."

Orla was on the floor lying in a heap, a thin trickle of blood running from her temple down the side of her face. But her eyes were fluttering open and she looked up at Wes and me.

"What… what happened?"

"I think it was this," Wes said, holding up a snow globe that said *Vegas* across the bottom.

I took it from him and turned it over, finding a smudge of blood that left no doubt as to whether it had been the weapon.

I dropped to my knees. "Orla, honey, are you okay?" I asked, smoothing her hair out of her face.

She touched her head and winced, but a pained smile spread across her face. "Go get her. Go get that bitch," she said in a wobbly voice

God, I loved her.

Shit. I loved her.

Leaving Orla with Wes, I took off in the direction Tige had run. At the end of the hallway was a narrow set of stairs, I imagined for household staff, confirmed when I reached the bottom of them and realized I'd ended up back in the kitchen. I glanced through the open door and saw Tige outside, having tackled the unfortunate Tawny.

I say unfortunate, because it was all over for the woman. No matter what she said now, she was screwed.

And Orla was cleared.

As soon as I stepped outside, Tawny's litany of indignant curses reached my ears. Tige had her pinned on her stomach, holding her hands behind her back with one hand, calling the police on his cell with the other.

"C'mon," Tawny pleaded. "Let me go. I'll make it worth your while. I have money in the Caymans. And I have ways to earn more."

I bet she did. Wonder who she'd frame next.

She squirmed violently in Tige's tight grip, coming to terms with the fact that her offer had failed to tempt him.

Her tone switched from bargaining to angry. "I did what I had to do," she screamed. "You would have done the same in my position. I never had a chance. No one ever gave me a chance... And because of your fucking nosiness, someone's trying to kill me now, too."

She continued wailing while the cops handcuffed her and I wondered if she should be grateful to be going to jail, where she was undoubtedly safer than she would be on the streets.

When the ambulance came for Orla, I waved them down and brought them right up to the room where she'd been knocked out. But being the badass that she was, she insisted on getting to her feet and descending the stairs on her own—with assistance, of course—before she was finally convinced by the ambulance crew that she had to lie down for them to take her to the hospital.

Before they loaded her in the back, Wes, Tige, and I gathered around her. We got some funny looks from the ambulance crew, but none of us gave a shit about that. We were focused on one thing.

I grabbed Orla's hand and kissed the back of it, bending closer to kiss her lips.

"Look at me," she said, with a small laugh. "I'm lying down, all strapped in, and you guys can't even enjoy me."

"Don't worry, baby," I said. "You'll have plenty of time to make it up to us later."

At the same time the ambulance drove away, so did the police car with Tawny in the back of it.

"That woman must be pretty familiar with jail," Wes said.

"No shit," Tige laughed. "She just keeps ending up back there."

We three stood there for a moment, I'd bet thinking mostly the same thing. It was Wes who had the balls to put it into words.

"Well. Was that the end of that?" he said to no one in particular.

Tige stared down at his shoes. "I was wondering the same," he said after a minute.

"I brought up to her the idea of being with us—all three of us—a while back. Maybe it's time to bring it up again," Wes added.

Fuck yeah.

We'd closed up the house as best we could and were heading to our car, lost in thought, when a limousine pulled into the circular drive. A sun-tanned, white-haired man jumped out and marched over to Tige, who was closest to him.

"What's going on here?" he demanded, pointing a finger. "This is my home, and you are trespassing."

Ah, Mr. Fellowes was back from safari.

The interesting thing was that, aside from the driver, there was no one else in the limo with him.

No *Mrs.* Fellowes.

Tige slowly approached him with an extended hand. "Mr. Fellowes. I am Tige St. James. Your daughter Orla hired our firm to help with a situation she found herself in."

Disbelief crossed the man's face. He had a lot of catching up to do.

He looked Tige up and down, then checked out Wes and me. Tige had grass stains and dirt on his white shirt, and Wes had a spot of blood on his. I was the clean one, for a change, but we were still a motley crew.

Mr. Fellowes turned back to Tige. "St. James? Are you a private detective? That St. James family?"

"I am sir. We all are." He introduced us and we shook hands with the man.

Tige continued. "In fact, I think you know my father."

Mr. Fellowes nodded slowly. "I do. I do indeed. So what the hell is going on here? Where is my daughter?"

"Sir, do you have time to talk? You've missed a lot while you were out of the country."

33

ORLA FELLOWES

"Hey, Dad."

I reached for my poor father, despondency covering his normally happy face. The guys had brought him to the hospital after briefing him on the whole story of what had gone on while he was away. He was a tough guy, but was not at all happy to see the condition I was in, especially when he found out Tawny had been the cause of the five stitches on my forehead.

"Jesus, Orla. You've been through the wringer. I'm so sorry, honey." He took my hand and pressed his forehead to mine like he did when I was a little

217

girl. It was comforting and heart-breaking at the same time. "I feel terrible I wasn't here to help. It's my fault. All my fault. I brought those people into our lives…"

I started to cry because, of course.

The guys, standing in the doorway, turned to leave.

But I waved them back. "No, no. You guys deserve to be here, just like Dad does," I said in my breaking, sniffly voice.

They returned slowly, letting Dad have center stage.

It was funny. There I was laid up in the hospital, and I was checking out their etiquette. But when it came to my dad, there was no leeway. If you weren't good to him, you were out. I did my best to make sure of it.

If the trash didn't take itself out, I took care of it.

"It's been a crazy couple weeks, Dad. You can't begin to know everything these guys did for me. They saved me. They really did."

Looking down at his hands, he shook his head slowly. "I don't know how I'll forgive myself for all this."

Whoa.

"There was no way you could know about Tawny, Dad. As for her mother—"

"She didn't come home with me," he said. "Your stepmother."

Oh my god. Where the hell was she?

"Wait. What?" I asked.

"Yeah. That's *my* big news. So now we're done with the two of them. Good riddance."

Holy crap.

"Dad, what happened?"

He rubbed his eyes. "Toward the end of the trip when we were back in Nairobi, I got an email from my banker asking why I was moving so much of my money out of the bank."

Oh no.

The guys looked at each other with their *heard that story before* expressions.

I took his hand. "Let me guess. *You* weren't moving the money."

With his lips pressed tightly together, he nodded.

Apollo stepped closer. "Sir, were the funds transferred to a bank in Grand Cayman by any chance?"

Dad nodded.

Holy shit. That horrible woman was fleecing my father while her daughter set me up. They were both criminals.

I was pretty much… speechless. Seriously. I think my mouth hung open so long, Dad handed me a cup of water.

It was all coming together. Both mother and daughter were grifters.

"Dad, I'm so sorry. I know this must be devastating for you."

As proud as ever, he shrugged. But I knew my dad, and like any other human, it hurt to be betrayed. "Well, she was a lousy travel companion, anyway."

I stifled a laugh, and when Dad caught me, he started laughing too. "When do you get out of this joint, honey?" he asked.

"First thing tomorrow if all goes as planned. They're keeping me overnight for observation. I guess they do that when you have a lump on your head."

He bent to kiss me on the head. "All right darlin'. If it's okay with you, I'll head home. Call me if you need anything. I need to get some sleep. I've been up for forty-eight hours straight. I'm so glad you're okay. And in good hands," he said, glancing at the guys.

"I'm glad you're okay too, Dad," I said, my voice cracking again.

He patted Apollo and Wes on the back on his way out. "Guys. Thank you for taking care of my daughter. I'll make sure you are well-compensated—"

Tige held a hand up. "Mr. Fellowes, that won't be necessary—"

But Dad waved him away. "Nonsense, son. I take care of people who take care of me." He turned back to me. "Let me know when you are ready to leave, honey. I'll come right over to get you. It will be nice to both be under the same roof again. We'll be home, Orla. You and me. Just like before. The way it should be."

As soon as he left, an awkwardness filled the room. It wasn't surprising. The whole reason for the four of us to be together was now gone.

What the hell were we going to do?

"So," Wes said, shuffling his feet. "Your dad was pretty clear about wanting you home."

I'd picked up on that, too.

Apollo sighed and grabbed the free chair next to my bed. "Guess there aren't many men out there who want their daughter shacking up with three men."

I supposed not. But still.

"He likes you guys. I can tell," I said.

"Then why don't you... you know... tell him," Wes said.

"Tell him what?" I asked, knowing the answer.

"*You* know, baby. You know," Tige said, his crooked smile beguiling the hell out of me.

34

ORLA FELLOWES

"Well, look who it is."

I plopped a big bag of croissants on Tige's desk as he, Wes, and Apollo eyed it hungrily.

Of course, after eyeing *me* hungrily.

And then I pulled an envelope out of my pocket and passed it to Tige. "From my father."

He clicked his tongue and with a fake-annoyed expression, peeked inside. His eyes widened, and he handed it back to me.

Rather, he tried to.

"This is crazy. Your dad doesn't owe us, much

less an amount like that. If anything, *we* should pay *you*."

Now that made me laugh.

I inched toward him in my flouncy flowered dress and red high heels. I finally had access to my closet again, and it felt damn good to have all my clothes back.

When I reached him, I leaned over and gave him a big kiss on the lips, favoring the side of my face with the bandage. "Just accept the payment. Dad won't take no for an answer. Use it for the vacation you had to cancel. Use it for a vacation for all four of us."

"I don't know, Orla—" he started to say.

But I interrupted. "Look. I'll never be able to thank you enough for all you did. What my dad is giving you there doesn't touch the appreciation I have. And, I'm kind of sad everything is coming to a close."

There. I'd said it. I knew I'd wanted to, but didn't know if I'd have the guts.

What I didn't elaborate on was the letdown of no longer having an excuse to live with them. Or, see them every day.

And that made me sad too

I turned to Apollo, whose eyebrows rose, and

then Wes, who looked me up and down with his sexy half-smile.

"Interesting you say that, Orla," Wes said.

"Say what?" I asked flirtatiously.

He sat on the edge of a desk and beckoned me with a finger. "That you mention, you know, *all four of us*. As in, use the money for a vacation *for all four of us*."

When I reached him, his giant hands wrapped around my waist, nearly encircling it. He pulled me close, and ran kisses down my neck.

My eyes fell closed as Apollo arrived to press against my back, essentially sandwiching me. Giant erections pressed against me on both sides, and I was dying to pull up my skirt and slip down my panties.

"Boys, boys," I said, "what a way to start the morning."

Apollo's hands slid up my thighs and, as if he read my mind, hooked his thumbs in the waistband of my panties and removed them. His hand immediately flew to my wet pussy, already throbbing with hunger.

In front of me, Wes unbuttoned my dress and reached for my tits, his thumbs roughing up my nipples before he took one in his mouth, drawing on it to the point of discomfort. I dropped my head back and moaned, engulfed in the delicious sensation of pleasure and pain.

"Step back, baby," Apollo said.

When I did, he easily bent me over so my head was essentially in Wes's lap, and my pussy was up in the air. I heard Apollo roll on a condom, and then he was at my entrance, pulsing into me as I tried to accommodate him.

At the same time, I'd pulled Wes's dick out of his pants, and began to lick and suck his swollen cockhead.

God, I needed this. I needed these men to make me feel good, and I needed to make them feel good in turn. I'd tossed and turned all night long in my room back at home, and no amount of pleasuring myself relieved the pressure between my legs. I was dying to be fucked and had waited up the rest of the night until the sun rose.

What had they done to me? I was like an unleashed monster, frantic about having escaped her cage. But instead of destroying everything in my path, I was relishing it. I had no fear about what lay ahead. I only saw the brightness of possibility.

Of course, that possibility wouldn't exist without the guys.

My guys.

As they were soon to find out.

In one swift moment, Apollo drove into me so deeply and filled me so completely that for a moment I couldn't breathe. I only remembered to when Tige spoke.

"Fuck her, man. Fuck her hard," he snarled in his dirty voice. "And suck that dick baby. Take Wes in your mouth all the way."

Not that we needed Tige to conduct our little orchestra, but there was no denying how hot it was to hear his rasping, growly voice express his desire. While I sucked Wes, and Apollo fucked me from behind, Tige reached under me and rubbed circles on my clit.

All three guys were working me, and I was in heaven. Pure heaven.

Wes was the first one to go. He gathered up all my hair in one fist and pushed his hips up toward my face. "Suck me, beautiful. I'm gonna unload in your mouth. Here it comes, baby. Here it comes."

His salty cum flooded my mouth with such fury I nearly choked, but I composed myself and swallowed it all.

Tige's strokes pushed me over my own edge, and as an orgasm slammed into me, so did Apollo behind me, holding my hips in a death grip while he unloaded.

After we'd caught our breaths, the guys stretched me out on the office sofa, my head in Tige's lap, my feet in Apollo's. Wes grabbed a blanket from the closet to cover me.

I was warm and cozy in seconds, and it was the most delicious feeling I'd ever experienced.

"So, guys," I said.

"Yeah?" Tige asked.

"I wanted to tell you that I think we can do it."

Fuck, I was taking a risk. I wasn't sure how they'd react. But I knew how I *hoped* they'd react.

"Do it? Do what?" Wes asked.

"You know. Be together."

There. I'd said it. Now to find out how they felt about it.

"I… thought this was something you didn't want," Apollo said.

I thought for a moment. "It wasn't that I didn't want it. I just didn't know how to make it work without hurting someone. But I feel differently now. I think we can figure shit out."

"What do you think your father will say?" Wes asked.

I knew this question was coming, but it was okay. I'd thought long and hard about it. The answer was, I had no answer. Only time would tell.

"We won't know until we run it past him. He

might approve, or he might not. But, you guys rank pretty high on his list right now. Seriously. He thinks the three of you can walk on water. And he was hinting around, asking if there might be some romantic interest brewing."

Wes shook his head. "Okay, but he's thinking of you with *one* guy. Not *three*."

Fair enough.

"I know. But he respects my judgment. And besides, he just left on a trip with his buddies. They're sailing around the world. Or something like that."

Apollo slapped his leg. "That guy is such a baller. Shit, I hope I'm like him when I'm that age."

"Well guys, the really good news is that he expects to be gone for a year or so and has asked me to watch the house. And the place is kind of big for me to bounce around in alone. So... I need housemates."

The room was silent for a moment as my proposal sank in. Then, in an explosion of delight, Wes pulled me to my feet and twirled me around, half dressed as I was, with Tige and Apollo laughing at his little-kid excitement.

When he set me down, I plopped back onto the sofa and took Tige and Apollo's hands. "So I have another job for you guys."

Tige shook his head hard. "No thanks. We'll stick to tailing cheating spouses and stuff like that. The art world is too crazy for our tastes."

Apollo held his hands up. "Hold on now. We haven't heard what the lady has in mind."

I jumped back up, pulling the blanket around me, and bounced up and down a little in my bare feet.

"How about you work under me, over me, beside me…" I giggled.

They rolled their eyes at my corny joke.

"You sure you want to see their ugly mugs every day?" Wes asked with a smirk, gesturing toward Tige and Apollo.

"Hey, fuck off, dude," Apollo said, flipping him off with a smirk.

Grabbing a croissant, I twirled around the room. "Look guys. I'm not going anywhere. I hope you're not, either."

I took a huge bite of the flaky, buttery delight.

I might not recognize whether art was real or not, but I knew we four had the real thing. That's all I really needed.

And wanted.

EPILOGUE

It didn't take Dad long to re-pack his bags and get the hell out of dodge.

But before he split, I sat him down and had a little talk.

"Hey, why don't you let me do that?" I asked.

He looked up from the cardboard shipping box he was sealing with tape, and sat back. He'd been at it all morning and even though he was glad to be done with my step-mother, I could see a hint of sadness in his eyes.

"Dad. You are an awesome guy. No more women for a while, though, okay? Enjoy your travels and give the ladies a rest."

He shook his head, laughed, and made no comment.

I didn't need another step-mother anytime soon.

My dad was a smart, strong man. He didn't become as successful as he had without some serious brains. But he was also a 'marrying man.' There was little he loved more than having a woman to come home to at the end of the day. He thrived when he had a partner to dote on and give lavish gifts to, someone to be on his arm for all the events and activities he attended, and a woman to remind him to take his high blood pressure medication and ensure he went to the gym.

But all that was behind him now, at least with regard to Tawny's mother, and to make sure there were no reminders of her around the house, he was personally packing up all her things.

Which he didn't need to do. He could get the house-keeper to do it. I'd even offered once or twice.

But I guess he saw the task as a sort of penance for bringing that woman and her criminal daughter into our lives.

And as for Tawny's 'brother' Jake? Yeah. She had no brother. Never had. As the guys had suspected, he was the one who facilitated the creation of the fake paintings, and used Tawny to get people to buy them. As soon as the heat was all over her, around the same time she tried to pin it all on me, he'd hit the road. Left no trace, apparently.

Poor Tawny. The grifter got grifted.

Now she knew what it felt like.

The problem was, he owed a bunch of people a bunch of money. When they couldn't find him, they came after her.

Oops.

But, lucky for her, the long arms of the art forgery world couldn't seem to penetrate the walls of the jail where she was being held—without bail—so she was safe.

For now.

Speaking of bail, I'd gotten all my money back, so I was no longer walking around with an empty bank account. Even better news was that I'd applied to the local school district for a kindergarten teacher job and things were looking good. Until that came through, I still had my job at St. James and Associates, which was now so inun-

dated with work that they were training new detectives. They desperately needed me to keep things organized, but I knew they'd also be glad to see me back in my happy place with snotty-nosed five-year-olds.

What could I say? I loved the little rugrats.

They also had some pretty freaking awesome artwork on their walls, thanks to the largesse of my dad. He felt so badly about what Tawny had done to the gallery's artists he bought up all their paintings.

The originals.

As for the copies, the guys finally found them. They hadn't been hidden in any sort of storage place, unless you consider my dad's basement one. That's right, Tawny had hidden the forgeries right in my dad's house in a dusty old storage room I don't think anyone had been in since we'd moved in. Wes had gotten a hunch about searching Dad's house and in particular, the basement.

It was so damn obvious, we all felt like idiots for not thinking of it sooner.

Apollo finally met with his dad, although he didn't do it in his office as Mr. Beck had requested. Instead, they met at a local coffee shop because that felt more neutral to Apollo. But he had nothing to worry about anyway. It was the same old shit he'd been hearing for years. Dad was giving him one more chance to make his family proud and pursue a 'real' profession.

That's right. Apollo's dad was nothing if not persistent.

But this time Apollo told him to hit the road, and I think for the first time ever, he didn't feel a bit of guilt about it. He'd accepted his father's limitations, and found they didn't need to limit him.

Jenni's wedding came off without a hitch, other than the ugly bridesmaid dress she made me wear. She wasn't mad at me at all, having gone missing during so much of her big event's planning. In fact, when I regained my footing, I realized she'd barely missed me. But when I asked if I could bring three dates to her wedding, well, that kind of got her attention.

Speaking of my three dates.

They were so handsome and attentive at Jenni's wedding, I was pretty sure I was the one who'd won the love jackpot.

Actually, I knew I had.

Tige was still talking about his longed-after kayaking vacation to the Sea of Cortez, so we'd planned a whopper of a trip for the four of us for next year. It was going to be first class all the way using the money my father had given the guys.

But to be honest, I'd be equally happy staying in a hut in the middle of Siberia with these men. Just so long as we were together.

Because what we had was about as far from fake as anything could get.

I hope you loved reading this book as much as I loved writing it. Please visit my store to learn more about my books, and to buy directly from me!

https://mikalaneshop.com/

ABOUT THE AUTHOR

Dear Reader:

I'm USA TODAY bestselling romance author Mika Lane, and am OBSESSED with bringing you sassy, steamy stories with imperfect heroines and the bad-a*s dudes they bring to their knees. I'll always bring you my signature humor and heat, topped off with a modern-day happily ever after.

My first book ever was *The Day I Ate the Milkyway*, a true fourth-grade masterpiece illustrated with crayons and bound with construction paper and glue. Nowadays, steamy romance gives purpose to my days and nights as I create worlds and characters that tickle the imagination. I live in magical Northern California with my own handsome alpha dude, sometimes known as Mr. Mika Lane, and two devilish cats named Chuck and Murray.

A dual citizen of the United States and Ireland, I have on more than one occasion spent my last dollar on a plane ticket somewhere, and am always planning my next escape. I often try new recipes on unsuspecting friends, search out hiding places to read undisturbed, and sadly kill every houseplant I bring home.

I LOVE to hear from readers when I'm not dreaming up naughty tales to share. Visit my online shop https://mikalaneshop.com/ and say hello https://mikalaneshop.com/pages/meet-mika.

xoxo, Mika

www.ingramcontent.com/pod-product-compliance
Lightning Source LLC
Chambersburg PA
CBHW011200190726
48286CB00009B/2860